CW00402357

CHAPTERS

1. Trapped
2. Dreamland
3. Rescue
4. Deal
5. Promise
6. Friends
7. Dreamland
8. Rescue
9. Tricks
10. Celebrity
11. Turns
12. Course
13. Overhear
14. Deal
15. Found
16. Help
17. Lost
18. Talk

22. Search
23. Report
24. Plan
25. Deal
26. Journey
27. Fair
28. Rescue
29. Gate
30. Rescue
31. Meeting
32. Ambush
33. Shot
34. Dreamland
35. Wait
36. Special

ILLUSTRATIONS

1. Max talks to Della
2. Luca crosses the Arches
3. Luca finds the squirrels
4. Luca and Barry
5. Barry looking the look
6. Luca leads the escape
7. Max holds the gate
8. Waiting for Max
9. My name's Max

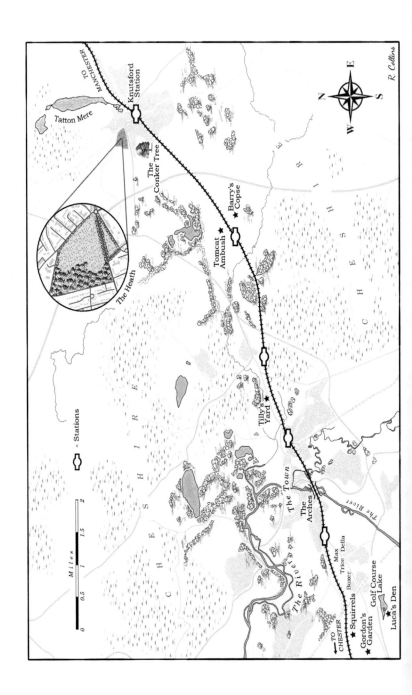

1. TRAPPED

So all day long the noise of struggle rolled among the bushes by the garden wall, at the back of the thick rhododendrons above the railway cutting.

Max the bull terrier was in a battle for his life, and it was a battle he was losing. He was never going to win. His thick stout leather collar was caught firmly on a thicker stouter rhododendron branch, that had been cut and coppiced close to the ground, and it was slowly strangling him. The more he fought, the tighter it became, and the bloodier the ring of bloody flesh round his neck. The more he struggled the more it tightened, and the more he fought the weaker he became.

All the garden animals knew what was happening – bird, cat, squirrel, hedgehog, and black mole underground – and each in his own way was sad or worried, neutral or exultant.

Jimmy and Jenny Squirrel, brother and sister, sat side by side in the angle of a branch high in a slender silver birch and looked down on the rustling and shaking bushes below them where Max was fighting for his life.

Occasionally during that long day and the dark night that followed a human would come out of the house or stand on the doorstep of the kitchen door at the back of the house and shout Max's name and whistle, and call, and sometimes bang a fork against his metal food bowl. But Max never came.

"I can't stand it," Jimmy said.

"But what can we do about it?" Jenny said.

"I'm not sure, nothing I expect," Jimmy said.

"No there's nothing we can do," Jenny agreed. "It's nothing to do with us."

"I don't know, maybe we should go and see what's happening. Maybe we can talk to him."

"Talk to him!" Jenny said. "Are you out of your mind?"

But she spoke to her brother's disappearing back. Jimmy was already scampering headfirst down the trunk of the silver birch towards the rhododendrons.

2. DREAMLAND

As the curtains of the night began to slide aside to reveal the first glimmers of a new morning, Max's struggles slowed and eventually ceased and finally he lay still. His breathing had shallowed almost to nothing. He lay in a trance, almost a coma of exhaustion. He was critically dehydrated and spent. He was near death.

And as he lay in this dream state, it seemed to him that a massive grey shape came shifting and drifting through the leaves and branches of the rhododendron bushes where Max lay trapped and which then seemed to coalesce into an almost familiar dog-like form and lie by Max's side, its massive head lying on its paws and its huge pale blue eyes looking down on him.

"Hello, Little Dog," a voice said in a soft murmur that seemed to come from inside Max's head. "If you can, be at peace," the voice whispered.

Somewhere deep in Max's semi-conscious mind the huge grey shape and the gentle voice triggered a recessive hidden ancestral memory. Could this be, was this, truly, Grey Wolf himself? The Ancestor, the First Dog, the Wolf-That-Was; the creator of the Contract?

"I cannot release you, Little Dog." Grey Wolf's deep voice passed silently into Max's mind. "But I can calm you and prepare you for what lies onwards. I can answer your questions."

"Are you Grey Wolf?" Max's mind asked the grey shape that now seemed to be all round him.

"I have many names, but some call me that. What my first name was, only my wolf-mother knew. But all dogs know me."

"What will happen to me?"

"There will be a silence, and everything you know will fade. There will be faint light, and you will move towards it. And I will be waiting in the light."

"And what then? What will I be?"

"Anything you wish. Everything you want."

There were so many questions, so many unknowns, so much that Max wished to know. "How did things come to be the way they are?" He asked. "Why am I not wild as other animals are? I'm not free like them. Why do I walk a kind of half-way world between the humans and other animals? What's it all about?"

The pale blue eyes of the great grey shape studied the bull terrier with a great and tender compassion. "You are here, Little Dog, because of what happened to me, what I did so many years ago; so many thousands of lives ago."

And Grey Wolf enveloped Max and Max dreamed. And he dreamed the story of Dogs and Man. The story of Grey Wolf and the human tribe, on a flat distant limitless steppe, where the caribou ran under a cold sharp sun.

"I was born in a time of struggle and conflict. It was a time of war. A war for space and food between my kind and the humans. We were rivals in a hard landscape. There were others, other humans of a different kind. The humans called them "the Heavies". And the humans competed with the Others for food and resources and sometimes fought against the Others. And the Others hunted my kind and drove us away wherever we met them. But the humans didn't behave that way. Sometimes they let us exist alongside them."

In his dream Max saw a group of humans with long wooden stone-tipped spears. He saw another group, thicker-set and more powerful, who also wore animal skins and furs, and similarly decorated their bodies with trinkets and trophies, but less skilfully and less beautifully, it seemed.

Max found the idea of two sets of different humans utterly astonishing. "Aren't they like gods?" His mind asked Grey Wolf. "They don't die. They don't change. They're gods?"

"They are powerful, it's true," Grey Wolf murmured. "But gods, no. Kind but capricious. Steadfast but untrustworthy. Honourable but multi-faceted. Not gods. Many of them nearer demons than gods. But I saw they held the key to the future for our kind. I saw that we could live with the humans. But not with the Others. They always hated us: but the humans did not always hate us."

And it seemed to Max that he entered the mind of the great grey shape lying all around him and he saw back in time. Back, back, back into a wild time. A time before gardens, before railway cuttings and before houses, before dinner bowls, before rhododendrons and brick walls. A time before cats and squirrels and all other domestic animals. A time of wildness and danger before things became tame. Back to a time of us and them. When us was a small family of humans living in a cave and them was everything else, and was either dinner or dangerous, or both.

And Max saw an animal, a large grey animal, Grey Wolf, the wolf-that-was. And Wolf-That-Was, unlike all other wolves, did not run away when the humans came near.

Outside the cave in the cliff face where the humans lived the ground fell away steeply through stunted ashes and birches and aspens to a broad shallow river, broken by shingle banks into a number of channels, and those in turn were interrupted by many stones with the streams guided and forced by larger boulders standing above the flow.

Across the river the grasslands began. The grass stretched away as far as the eye could see. In the distance, many many days' journey away the mountains emerged from the plain into purple foothills and high green pastures; and above the green was black rock and above all else, great snow-capped heights. Nearer to hand small streams etched deep narrow valleys into the level plane of the grass. These running clefts were used by the humans of the cave as their killing ground.

Herds of huge herbivores, elk and bison and aurochs, the great wild cattle of Palaeolithic times, the Old Stone Age 30,000 years ago, roamed the grasslands. And the humans of the cave hunted them by driving pockets of the herds over the low cliffs of the rivulets that crossed the plains. The men of the cave butchered and divided up the carcasses there, and feasted for days at a time in temporary skin-covered shelters by the stream banks and brought much of the animal meat and remains home by means of man-hauled skin and wood carrying frames called travois to the cave where the young women and the old men and women waited, guarding the children of the three-generation broad extended family.

When all that could be taken from the animals was taken, the meat for food and bones for tools and sinew for other tools, and skins for clothes and bedding, the leftovers were thrown down the cliff face below the cave entrance.

There, among the aspens and birches, wolves came and

searched the remains and found that it was good. And when the humans came down from the cave the wolves disappeared like grey ghosts into the trees and lay hidden till the humans went away. And in time the attraction of the field of human debris and detritus and waste became so large and strong that a family of wolves took up permanent residence at the base of the cliff below the cave among the aspens and the birches. And in time as the generations came and went the wolves became less wary of the humans, and though they kept much distance between themselves and the humans, the distance was less than it used to be in the generations before. And there came a time when one wolf, the Wolf-That-Was, did not run away at all when the humans approached.

A day's journey from the human cave, in another cave in the same bluff above the same river lived a large group of what the humans called the Others, or more often the Heavies for they were bigger and larger and stronger than humans. They too hunted the large animals of the plain. And they too brought large parts of the carcasses home to their cave to feed the women and children and to make tools and clothes and weapons from the animal remains. And below the Heavies' cave they too created an area of rubbish and debris where wild animals, wolves especially, but also the great long-toothed tiger cat, came and found things good to eat.

Unlike the humans, the Heavies killed these animals when they could and drove them away from the debris area at the base of their cliff. For wolf skin made the best winter clothes and the great incisor teeth of the tiger-cat was much prized as a decoration by the hunters; and their women feared and detested these predators as children killers. And no group of wolves were ever allowed to make a home near the debris below the Heavies' cave. And time went by and these two groups, the humans and the Heavies, became set in their ways.

Winters came and went; and winters were hard. Snow came, spreading down from the far mountains and covered the grassland, and many of the large herd animals of the plain, the elk and the bison and the aurochs, moved south for the winter to where the snow lay thinner on the ground or did not come at all. And on the plain across the river the only prey animal in winter was the caribou which came in great herds from the north and they remained and lived on the dead grass below the snow through the winter. And the wolves and the other predators followed the herds south. But Wolf-That-Was and his family did not go south with the other wolves. They stayed the whole winter through in their den in the aspens below the cave in the bluff where the humans lived and fed on the leftovers in the debris field among the trees.

Now it turned out that the humans were more skilful than the Heavies at killing the great grass-eaters of the plain. There were fewer of them, but they were better organised. They seemed to be better able to make a plan for killing, and to stick to it. It was them who first understood that small elements of the herd could be ambushed and separated from the rest and driven with spears and arrows and fire to their death over the low cliffs of the rivulets of the plain. The Heavies watched from their high cave and understood and copied this method. But they had not thought of it for themselves. And the Heavies were not always successful.

In summer when prey was plentiful this difference did not matter. There was plenty of food to be caught or trapped or driven over the cliffs. But winter was a different story. Then when only the hard-to-kill caribou remained it seemed that the humans were more successful more often and took more of the available food. And many days the Heavies went hungry.

And there came a time when the Heavies became desperate. Their children were becoming weak and diseased through lack of food. And winter was long and hard and cold and seemed unending. And they began to wonder why should they starve when the new people were full of food and stayed healthy? They were the first people in this land. The others were newcomers, arriving uninvited to their lands, living in their caves, taking their birthright, killing their food. The Heavies were bigger and they were stronger and they feared nothing. And the Heavies living in the cave in the bluff above the river began to understand that if they could drive the humans away the food that remained would be theirs alone to hunt. And who knew also how human-child might taste? Might it not be good to eat?

The mother-chief of the Heavies of the cave made a plan.

The cave of the humans was a day's journey away. She would send her hunter-men against them. The hunters were big and muscular and very powerful. Much bigger and much more powerful than the hunters in the human cave family. There were perhaps twice as many of them than there were of the newcomers. She would send a large group of her hunters to kill the newcomers. They would journey stealthily along the river until they came at night to the cave of the humans. During the night they would lie hidden below the cave. And as first light came, and as the humans still slept, they would rush up and in to their cave and attack them and kill them all and butcher and cook and eat their children. And all the herds of caribou on the winter plain would be theirs to hunt, as they had hunted the herds for a hundred thousand years before the newcomers came.

After night fell the Heavy hunters reached the section of the river below the humans' cave. They made their way silently into the first trees on the rising slope and found places to hide. They set a watch and slept.

Before dawn the last sentinel roused his fellows. They prepared for battle by painting their faces with red ochre. Then with a gesture from their leader they took their spears and crept silently up the steep slope. There was no sound from the cave above. It seemed that all the occupants were still asleep.

Suddenly all hell broke loose. A cacophony of urgent animal warning sounds split the early dawn.

Wolf-That-Was had been aware of their presence from the night before. He knew that a party of the deadly dangerous other-humans, had arrived in the vicinity and was sleeping not far below his den near the humans' rubbish field. Unsure whether to stay or flee, he had not slept the entire night. Then with the first light of dawn he was instantly aware that these other-humans were on the move up the slope towards his den. He could be silent no longer. He raised his snout to the moon, still high in the early morning sky, and let forth a piercing noise that seemed to all who heard it to be a series of interconnected barky howls. All the animal's fear and worry and alarm was contained in the sound, and all who heard it, animals and men, for a mile or so around became instantly awake.

Danger! Danger! Enemies! Danger! The sound said. Soon all Wolf-That-Was's family and litter mates joined in the racket.

Among those awoken by the ear-splitting noise were the light-sleeping human hunters resting in the cave above. Two men instantly woke and rose and pushed aside the large aurochs skin curtain that covered the entrance to their cave and peered down the slope to see what the noise was. They were just in time to see a group of Heavy hunters leave the cover of the trees and begin to charge up the remaining fifty or sixty yards to the mouth of the cave.

The distance was far enough to give sufficient time for the two humans to rouse the rest of their fellow hunters, to arm themselves with flint-tipped spears, skilfully shafted stone axes and clubs, tear down the aurochs skin and form a defensive line across the mouth of the cave.

Despite being outnumbered two-to-one the seven human defenders of the cave had the advantage of higher ground, knowledge of the terrain, and the fact that the fight would be in a tight space. They also had a previously unknown and untested advantage: their weapons were longer, sharper, straighter and better made and more deadly than their opponents'. The humans too had a technological advantage over the Heavies. They possessed the spear-thrower and the Heavies did not. The humans' spears were designed to be thrown, and the spear-thrower added great distance and great power to the flight. The spears possessed by the Heavies were designed and used for stabbing and thrusting only, with their great power and weight behind them. They never threw them.

By this means the humans were able to kill two of the Heavy attackers and wound another even before they came within stabbing distance of the cave.

The fight was short, sharp and very deadly. For the cost of one human dead and another badly injured, the Heavies lost five men dead and two more horrifically wounded before the rest gave up the fight and ran back down the slope through the trees to the river, dragging another of their wounded with them.

There were two results of the battle of the cave mouth. The Heavy survivors returned to their cave. Soon afterwards the mother-chief of the Heavies decided they must move away from the area to find or create a new home in new pastures where they hoped the competition for food from the newcomers would be less or non-existent. Nothing was heard from them again.

The other result was a full and proper understanding by the humans of the cave that they owed their survival that day to the warning given by the family of wolves that lived around their rubbish dump at the base of the slope below their cave. For the first time they began to understand that the presence of the nearby wolf family, hitherto no more than tolerated, might be a real asset. And they began to take a closer interest in the wolves and their well being.

Thus was the alliance, the symbiosis, the contract, begun between humankind and the animal that became the dog.

Soon the humans noticed that any stranger, friend or foe, human or animal, approaching their cave was heralded by urgent howling-barks from the wolves below. Not just Heavies but also other bands of fellow humans could be deadly enemies in the competition for space and food and resources in those times. And not a few times over the years and generations of their occupation of the cave were the humans attacked by other groups of humans; and yet never once were they surprised or caught napping by a raiding party. They were always given warning by the wolves. And, as everyone knows, to be forewarned is to be forearmed.

There was another of Wolf-That-Was's genes in action among the rubbish-tip wolf pack as well as the one that allowed a minimum flight distance in the presence of humans. This was what can best be described as an equality gene. Wolf packs generally form a strict hierarchy, a pack, with an alpha male and an alpha female at the head and subordinate males and females ranked below. But with the pressure exerted by the equality gene inherited from Wolf-That-Was, the rubbish-tip pack became more of a gang or band than a pack. The alpha male and female, though they still ruled the gang for many generations, became more of first-among-equals than true dominant alphas. And over time the hierarchy structure died away completely leaving a new kind of animal, the wolf-dog with a new way of behaving where each member of the gang was the equal of any other member of the gang. And all members of the gang supported the gang and promoted its well-being.

And on occasion when a wolf-mother succumbed to an early death through injury or disease, her pups would be cared for by the other members of the rubbish-tip gang. Then once in one great long and harsh winter, the alpha wolf mother was killed and the beta mother badly injured in a hunt with a strong and vigorous caribou. And afterwards the beta mother could only feed the alpha mother's pups, as wolf ways and genes demanded. And though the equality gene inherited from Wolf-That-Was allowed the beta mother to produce a litter at the same time as the alpha mother, in the absence of the alpha mother the beta mother could not feed her own pups and so they were cast out and abandoned. And so they were found and taken in and cared for by the humans in the cave above the rubbish tip.

And those pups grew to adulthood and they did not return to the rubbish-tip-pack, for they all carried the gene of their ancestor Grey Wolf, the Wolf-That-Was, who did not run away when humans approached. Instead they stayed with the humans, their adopted family gang, throughout their lives; as did their offspring and all their generations after them. And they guarded the cave and helped with the hunt and did all the other things. And so the contract between wolf-dog and man that had started with Grey Wolf's warning cry so many generations before was finally sealed.

In his dream before death came Max began to understand his place in the universe.

But suddenly in Max's mind the grey in turn was replaced by the grey. Not a great grey wolf shape this time, but a smaller much smaller grey shape with a tail that floated in the air and which seemed to flow like a furry stream into the places where the rest of the body had been a moment before.

3. RESCUE

Up in the branches of the silver birch above the rhododendrons the squirrel had come to a decision.

"I've had enough of this. It's too quiet. I'm going down to see what's going on." Jimmy began to descend the tree.

"You can't. Come back," Jenny called after him, but Jimmy was gone. Jenny followed, more slowly.

Jimmy carefully climbed down the trunk of the silver birch and peered into the depths of the rhododendron bush. He could see nothing. He descended further, beneath the budding pink flowered canopy of the bush. In the gloom below what he saw was a medium-sized powerfully built black, brindled and white-patched dog lying on his side on the ground. His thick leather collar was twisted round his throat, and Jimmy could see it was caught on the stout stub of a broken branch of the bush near the ground. The dog was barely breathing. Foam speckled the line of his mouth and a bloody imprint round his throat marked the line of his collar.

Jimmy approached. He climbed up the base of the rhododendron and stood on the thick branch from which the dog's collar was suspended.

Afterwards Jimmy could never say why he did what he did that day. Perhaps he never knew why he did it. Sure, he made up stories full of bravado about what he did, with himself as the hero and central character, as squirrels always do, but the truth he never admitted even to himself. And that was that Jimmy felt sorry for the trapped animal, big and deadly and dangerous as he was. Jimmy felt an overwhelming urge to help the trapped animal; to release him if he could.

Jimmy crouched down and examined the situation more closely. He knew he wasn't behaving like a squirrel should. But there was something else, something new that made him do things differently. He tried to pin it down in his mind, but it flitted away, elusive like a squirrel itself. Jimmy let it go. Then he took a deep breath, and turned to the matter in hand. He began to chew through the thick leather collar that had caught and trapped and was killing the dog.

The squirrel's razor sharp teeth made rapid inroads into the leather. In less than a minute the collar was severed. The collar fell away from the branch where it was caught, and the dog's head, now released, sank gently to a more comfortable position on the ground. The dog began to breathe easily again.

Immediately as he chewed through the last millimetre of the collar and the dog was released, Jimmy sprang upwards into the bush, putting a safe distance between him and the dog. He jumped from the rhododendron across to the trunk of the silver birch and disappeared up into the heights of the tree where Jenny was waiting. He didn't notice as he did so the half-open eyes of the exhausted dog watching him go.

4. DEAL

Some days later, when a great deal of Max's strength had returned, but the bloody welt on his neck had not yet healed, Max the bull terrier stood below a silver birch and sniffed up into the tree.

Up in the high branches Jimmy and Jenny looked down at the dog.

"Uh-oh," Jenny said. "Look what you've done. We've got trouble now."

Then Max said something that had never been asked by one of his kind to one of the squirrel kind before. He asked. "Well, O Squirrel, I know you're there. I can't see you, but I can smell you. I want to talk to you, and above all I want to ask you something. Is there anything I can do for you? You did a great thing for me. Now I'd like to repay that."

"Interesting," Jimmy said. "What do you make of that?"

"It's a trap, obviously. You can never trust a dog."

"I'm not so sure in this case. You heard him." Jimmy began to move head first down the trunk of the tree, ignoring the calls of "Wait, wait, what're you doing? You're mad."

Eventually Jimmy came to the lowest branch of the tree, in sight of the dog but still well above his reach. He knew it would be out of reach even of the lively Trice from the other side of the wall; and even inaccessible to the incredibly springy boxer-dog from two gardens away. And he thought the dog below looked nothing as springy as those two, powerful as he clearly was. Jimmy sat on his haunches on top of the branch and looked down.

"Hello Dog," he said, quietly but with the confidence of a safe distance between him and the dog.

"Hello," Max said, his voice husky. "Was it you or your friend who released me?"

"It was me. Jimmy Squirrel, the one and only, at your service." Squirrels can never be serious for long.

"Well thank you Jimmy Squirrel. My name is Max. I'm a bull terrier dog."

"Well you don't look much like a bull, and I'm not sure what a terr-i-er is," Jimmy said nonchalantly. "But I'm clear with the dog angle."

Max laughed hoarsely. "You might be right at that," he said. "Why did you do it?"

Jimmy knew what he meant and knew what he was being asked, and momentarily he almost returned a flippant answer. But then understood a serious question was being asked that required a serious and thoughtful answer, hard as that was for a squirrel to do.

Many thoughts went through Jimmy's mind; many phrases that sounded wise and intelligent and philosophical. Things like, "It was something so easy for me to do, yet so hard for you." And "I wanted to show I could control things." And "I wanted to see myself as an all-action hero."

But he said none of these things out loud to the dog.

He just said: "You don't always have to do what you're supposed to." And with those words Jimmy realised for the first time himself what that elusive feeling had been, and what he had felt, when he had decided impulsively to chew through the dog's collar.

Max cocked his head on one side, as though not sure what the words meant or implied.

"Does that answer your question?" Jimmy said.

"Er, yes, I think it does." To Max the idea of an animal purposefully not doing what they were supposed to do as that kind of animal was exceedingly strange. He realised these little grey phantoms were complex animals.

"Having said all that," Max said with a tone that implied things were getting too complex and it was time to move on, "I'd like to know if there's anything I can do for you?"

The words hung in the air, and it took a while before Jimmy realised the dog was actually offering to do something for the squirrels. Vast schemes and heroic plans and phantasms crammed through Jimmy's mind. But he forced them away. This clearly was an opportunity he could not afford to miss.

Both animals were silent for a minute. Then the squirrel spoke again.

"Well," said Jimmy. "There's a cat."

5. PROMISE

"Hello, O Cat, I'd like to talk to you."

Max talks to Della

Della the big white cat stopped, startled. It was a long time since any animal had tried to talk to her, apart from little birds pleading for their lives. And she'd never been addressed by a dog before, especially not in the slightly comical Old Common Speech. Normally they just made silly futile and aggressive barking and growling dog-noises.

"Well, O Dog, I can think of nothing we can possibly have to say to each other," she said dismissively and made to move further along the top of the garden wall, rudely showing her backside and waving her large fluffy white tail at him.

"Hold on, Cat," Max said, dropping into the rude vernacular version of the Old Common Speech, a rudeness worsened by the hoarseness and deepness of Max's voice, due to his still-sore throat caused by the vicious constrictions of his collar in his recent struggle with the stout rhododendron branch. "Stop and talk right now, or someday, sometime, somewhere I'll seek you out and track you down and I'll catch you and I'll bite your arse. I guarantee, Cat, you'll listen to me then."

The cat stopped, reluctantly and looked down at the rude and vile dog. It never did to underestimate a dog's threats, empty as they usually were.

"Now Cat, you may not think I will ever be able to catch you, and you may be right at that, and you may therefore think you're safe from me. But my friend Trice is a different story, isn't she?" Trice was a friend of Max's. She was a young incredibly lively and fast border collie who lived next door on the other side of the brick wall, where she chased anything that moved in her domain, on the ground, in trees and even in the air. "A word from me and she can make your life tiresome and very much a misery, can she not?"

Della the white cat thought about this for a while. What the slow-solid burly-sturdy dog was saying was true. In winter Trice lived indoors with her pack of humans, and the cat could roam her garden all night unmolested; but in the summer she spent the nights in an open shed in the garden. A word from Max and Trice's huge inviting enticing exciting almost wild gardens and paddock would more-or-less be out of bounds to the cat. She wouldn't like that at all. No more oh-so-satisfying stalking and pouncing and ambushing of little creatures. Instead she'd always be on the lookout for a bouncy dog sprinting at her with intent to chase and chastise.

"That's better," Max said as the cat sat down on the top of the wall about nine feet above him and begin licking her paws in a show of distance and unconcern.

"Now then," Max said moving into normal speech after the polite initial greetings of the Old Common Speech. "There are some new facts of life I wish to discuss with you. I understand you've been troubling the lives of some friends of mine, and that has made me consider your behaviour and your freedom of action in my domain a little more closely than I have done in the past. And now after some thought on this matter, I have some new rules, which you will be wise to obey. In fact you will obey these new rules on pain of death."

"I'm afraid I don't understand you," the white cat said, seriously alarmed and stalling for time, and becoming, for the first time, unusually polite.

"Then I'll speak even more plainly. I'm going to tell you how you will in future behave in my domain. From now on if you fail to stick to these rules of behaviour, I will kill you." He looked up at the cat. She was listening now, very hard.

"Killing is what I do," Max continued. "And when I choose I do it even better even than you do. You may be a natural killer, but for all that you remain just that, a natural. You remain an amateur in that you kill to play and sometimes kill to eat, no more than that. You do it because you do it. I, on the other hand, am a professional. You do what you do because you were born that way. But I was designed to kill. I enjoy it. You kill to live. I live to kill."

The white cat was clearly shaken but tried not to show it. "What new rules are these?" she said throatily.

"I've watched you, and am aware of your terrorising and tormenting the small animals here and around this neighbourhood. But it is not my place to comment on that or to criticise. That is your way, and the way of your kind. Now some of my kind, such as my friend Trice, would chase you and chase you whenever they saw you, that is their way. But it is not my way. I fight and I kill, but I don't chase. Therefore you have been able to pursue your way in my domain quite freely with no interference from me." Max paused and looked up at the cat again. "However from this day forward all that will change." Dog and cat looked at each other in silence for a long moment.

"Here is the new rule," Max said. "From now on here in this garden you will kill no living thing. Neither will you play with nor torment nor torture any living creature here. You may pass through, and thou may defecate and urinate here, and do all else here that you may wish to do following your way. But you may not kill nor maim nor torment here, whether that be your way or not. Above all, here in this garden you will not kill, harm, injure, chase or ambush, torment or torture any squirrel." Max could see the cat understood exactly what he was saying.

He carried on: "And be aware that I need not actually see you breaking this rule. I will know you and your actions, and what you've done, by your smell. Apart from this, you may come and go and move freely as you wish. Yet know that if you break this rule or attempt to bend it in any way, I will hunt you and I will find you and I will catch you and I will kill you. Do you understand?"

The big white cat looked down at the burly sturdy powerful dog she despised so much. She looked at the huge jaws and the massive muscular neck and she imagined being caught by those jaws and being ragged and jerked side to side in a fraction of a second by that muscular neck until her own neck or back broke, then being tossed disdainfully aside, dead before she hit the ground. And she looked at the long snout with its incredible sense of smell that would know her and her actions, and which would track her down and find her wherever she lay hidden. And she knew that nowhere would she be safe. And for the first time in her carefree pampered but semi-wild life she was afraid.

"Cat, do you understand?" Max repeated.

"Yes, Dog, I understand," she answered coldly, but clearly. And then, despite her attempt to remain haughty and unaffected, she asked: "Why Dog? Why has this come about?"

"I have a debt of honour. And this is just a small attempt to begin to repay what can never be repaid. Now Cat, go about your way."

"Go about your way too, Dog," Della the cat replied and sauntered away, apparently unchanged and carefree along the top of the garden wall.

6. FRIENDS

Max and the squirrels regularly began to meet and talk. Jimmy was always on the lookout for a chat with his new friend, and Jenny too gradually overcame her caution and came down from the higher reaches of the silver birches to say hello. From them Max learned a lot more about the neighbourhood than he had known before. Sure, he'd travelled much further than any of the garden animals because he'd been on journeys in cars, but he could never say he got to know the places he'd passed by and through. Even sticking his head out of the window and sniffing the passing air was more frustrating than helpful. But he'd never had the freedom to roam the land and gardens around as the squirrels did.

They told him of all the neighbourhood dogs. The labrador three houses away in a certain direction: "Yes, I've heard her barking," Max said: and the old spaniel, much housebound who lived much further away in another direction. The springy boxer-dog not far away. And then there was Trice the sheepdog on the other side of the garden wall.

"I almost asked you if you could do something about her," Jimmy said. "When you first came to the bottom of the tree and asked to talk to us. She's a menace. She doesn't stop. She never catches us, but she never stops trying."

"Then I'm afraid I would have refused. She is what she is. And also she is a friend of mine. I cannot ask her to change her ways in her own garden."

"I knew that," Jimmy said.

"Are there any dogs around like me?" Max asked one time. "A bull terrier?"

"You mean a bully-terrier? I'm sure the cat thinks that." Jimmy squeaked with laughter at his own joke.

"No, none like you," Jenny said.

That's a pity, Max thought.

Another time Jimmy asked Max why he didn't chase squirrels and birds and cats and anything that moved in his garden, like Trice did in hers.

"Because they don't fight," Max said. "They just run. Who's

interested in aimless chasing when you never catch anything? Not me. I like fighting. I don't fruitlessly chase and never catch. What's the point in that? Me I'm a fighter. I'm a killer. In fact I'm often a dog-killer. Though I also do have to say that when the white rage comes upon me I'll kill anything and everything. I won't stop."

He said it so proudly and matter-of-factly the squirrels were shocked. They had got used to this polite bully-terrier who wanted to talk to them and help them. They had forgotten how dangerous and lethal he was. He was a killing machine, and knew it. And liked it.

Another time, less seriously, the dog and squirrels were talking about their names for other animals. Max told them of the nicknames dogs have for all other animals according to their excrement – by action, size, shape, colour and smell. So rabbits are "Pea-Shooters". Squirrels are "Streakers" (the squirrels thought this was a reference to the way they moved, until they realised what Max was really talking about). Birds are "Limers". Cows are "Sloppers". Cats are "Buriers" or "Stinkers" (that's because cat crap really does stink even for dogs, Max explained). Horses are "Movers" because apart from birds they are the only animal that craps while they're moving. And then the great mystery: humans are "No-Turds" because no dog has ever seen human turds, therefore they are a great unknown.

"We have a saying in the dog world: he's okay, but his shit doesn't stink." And Max made a strange wheezing noise through his nose, which much mystified the squirrels until they realised this was Max laughing.

"I never realised this subject was so interesting," Jenny said ironically.

"Information. Information. Information," Max replied. "By smelling your waste I can tell what animal you are; what sex you are; where you live; what direction you're going; where you come from; how healthy you are; how dangerous you are; how much of a rival and competitor you are; and whether I can eat you or not."

"So, knowledge is power?" Jimmy said. "All animals have strengths and weaknesses. We can climb and we're amazingly acrobatic. But we can't get information like you can through your nose. But cats can climb and you can't. And so on."

"Yes, it's all a balance. Everything's in balance."

"But I think sometimes they" – he gestured towards the house over Max's shoulder – "Upset the balance," Jimmy said.

"That's my family-band you're talking about," Max said. "Leave it out."

The squirrels looked at each other, confused. How could this dog foolishly imagine he was a human? Why was he pretending he was part of a human family?

Later they talked more about it.

"I think Max really does think he's part of a human family," Jimmy said. "I'm not saying he's actually under the delusion that he is a human. But he does live in the house with them. So I don't know."

"Do you think he lives there without the humans knowing?" Jenny suggested. "You know, like mice and rats do."

"No. I don't think that's it. I think instead it's some kind of weird special relationship."

"At any rate he's very protective of them."

"Yes that's true. Maybe he can tell us some more about this 'special relationship' another time."

7. DREAMLAND

Max was sleeping in the sun. He'd spent a large part of the morning investigating the interesting smells along the top of the railway cutting at the bottom of his garden. Access was easy; a line of shrubs marked the end of his humans' property, and all that prevented access to the steep trench of the cutting was a long section of old iron fencing, originally painted black and white, but now much rusted and in a poor state of repair.

This was the Cheshire Lines railway. The line was quiet. Trains ran only one an hour or so in both directions, to Manchester northeastwards and westwards to Chester. Railway lines are the great arteries by which wild animals move around the country.

Max eased his way through the shrubs and slender drooping willow trees, ducked under the lowest band of the iron fencing and began to check out with his nose what had been happening recently along the top of the cutting. Squirrel-smell he recognised, and there was a lot of that smell along the railway line. Fox too he knew. He'd never actually seen the fox Luca himself, but he knew all about him from the scents he left.

There were other smells too, rabbit, bird, mole and now something else, something new. Max had never smelled this one before, but the information his nose was bringing to his brain indicated a quite large animal, a slow-moving ground dweller, in good health, probably nocturnal. Max had never seen a badger, but if he eventually did, such was the certainty he placed in the information received through his nose that the visual sighting would be no more than mere confirmation of the picture he had already built in his mind.

Max wandered forty yards or so at a leisurely pace along the top of the railway cutting, then stopped and retraced his steps. He knew where his territory ended, and he knew the hazards of penetrating uninvited into another dog's domain. But something more than that always prevented him crossing the imaginary line and wandering further along the railway. He knew he wasn't supposed to. He knew, in various ways, that his humans didn't want him leaving the garden. It wasn't really anything specific. He just knew that they didn't want him to wander far. So he didn't. He could feel when they talked to him about it that they felt it was all for his own good. He didn't understand exactly what they were saying, but he understood it was fundamental to his being part of the family, and that the curb was intended to keep him from harm. And while Max always felt he could look after himself, come what may, an urge even stronger than the urge to follow a scent always made him stop at the border and go no further; and that was the urge to please his humans, his family, his band.

There was a sandy patch at the far western border of his domain, where a large sycamore tree hung over the cutting and a broad soft sandy area lay exposed underneath it. In time gone by a rope had been attached to the largest lowest branch of the tree and a swing made. Children swung on the swing and played and dug holes in the sand. That was long before Max's time, and now the fraying rope hung idly swaying in the wind and children no longer played in the sand.

This was one of Max's favourite places. The sandy area acted as a sun-trap and there was a particular spot against a high bank where the sand mingled with the exposed roots of the tree where Max always chose to lie down and watch the world go by and sleep awhile.

He still had a very nasty grazed area on his neck, though it was mending fast. And he dreamed again of the time of the wolves and the ancestor dogs. It seemed that again the great grey wolf lay alongside him in the sandy den lined with tree roots, his great grey head lying on his paws.

But now as Max dreamed it seemed that the grey shape grew fainter and a new shape grew stronger in its place. "Hello Max," a vibrant, gleeful, wild whisper entered his ear and coursed vividly round his body. The grey was replaced by the white, as a huge lean white shape laid its head next to Max and looked at him with excited laughing bright red eyes.

"Come with me," the voice said. "And kill. Be yourself. Be everything you ever wanted to be. Kill. And fight and kill. Be a hero. Be the champion you really are. Come with me, push the boundaries and explore," the whisper urged again.

Dim dark images flickered and distant echoes rumbled in the

deepest parts of Max's consciousness.

Instinctively, as with Grey Wolf, at a subliminal level Max knew to whom the great white shape and gleeful voice belonged. This was Albion. The Outsider. White Wolf, Wild Wolf. The Old One. Grey Wolf's litter-mate and brother had many names.

"Are you White Wolf, the Wild One?" Max's mind asked the white shadow.

"Don't listen to him," the voice said. "My grey brother. He only tells half the story. And yes, my wolf-mother called me Albion," he added.

And again Max dreamed. He saw the same vast great grassland plains stretching away to the distant purple mountains. He saw the bluff overlooking the river with the cave of the humans. He saw the hunters from the cave driving the great grass-grazers over cliffs into the deep rivulet valleys that crossed the plain. But now he saw something new. The hunters were being helped by wolves. But they weren't quite wolves. The three animals that Max saw in his dream were not as big as a wolf but bigger than a coyote. Yet they looked and sounded and acted like wolves. Max guessed they were wolf-dogs, somewhere in between wolves and dogs.

And it seemed to Max that the wolf-dogs were doing most of the work in this new style of hunting. The wolf-dogs ran at and charged the elk herd and by this means identified a young inexperienced mother and her calf. Then working together the wolf-dogs skilfully separated out the mother and calf from the herd and began to drive the prey towards the edge of a small cliff perhaps a mile away across the plain. Max saw that a line of fur-clad human hunters were standing close to the edge of the cliff. They were armed with spears and bows and arrows and were lighting large firebrands. It was only at the last minute, as the mother and calf hesitated on the brink of the cliff, that the humans joined the hunt. Now charging towards them from behind and shouting, the six hunters threw spears and waved their firebrands at the terrified animals, who turned and plunged to their deaths down the cliff face and lay, broken-backed and broken-necked, kicking their death-throes in the shallow stream below.

In his dream Max watched as the humans climbed down the

cliff into the stream bed and began to skin and butcher the carcasses. And then Max saw something that chilled him to the bone. One of the wolf-dogs approached the calf carcass which a hunter was beginning to skin. Immediately the hunter rose and shouted at the wolf-dog and beat it with the flat of his spear and chased it away. The wolf-dog ran away to a safe distance, its tail between its legs.

And Max saw that hours later when all the butchering was done, the hunters threw a couple of small pieces of skin to the waiting wolf-dogs, who fought for it among themselves, with the smallest wolf-dog having nothing.

Just pieces of skin! Max was shocked. After all that work! And what was most shocking was the wolf-dogs seemed grateful for such small pickings. They followed the hunters and their travois at a respectful distance all the way back to the cave. And there Max saw that the wolf-dogs were not allowed to enter into the cave. They were forced to stay outside, hungry in the cold. And he saw that if a wolf-dog dared to peer into the cave, stones were thrown at him, and if he persisted a man or a woman would emerge from the cave and beat the wolf-dog with a stick or the shaft of a spear.

It seemed to Max that a clear pack hierarchy was being forced on the wolf-dogs by the humans, and the wolf-dogs had to learn to adapt to this now unnatural old way and shake off and lose their own natural band-of-brothers-and-sisters gang-equality. And yet the wolf-dogs still stayed round the cave. It seemed they had nowhere to go to. It seemed they had forgotten how to leave.

"It's true," the silky gleeful voice said in Max's mind. "That's what became of the so-called 'contract' your beloved Grey Wolf established with the humans." The word humans was hissed with extreme hate and loathing. "We, the great wolves, became underdogs. We became no more than slaves."

Much troubled, Max pondered all these things.

And in his dream he saw a beautiful lean white wolf leave the rubbish-tip pack and make a new life for himself on the plain. He interacted with other wolves and joined at times other packs and fathered many offspring, some great lean white red-eyed wolves like their father. But he and they never had any dealings with humans. He shunned them and avoided them and hated them with all his fierce heart.

"Trust no human," the white wolf whispered. "Break the contract and live."

Slowly Max felt the presence of the white wolf fading away, and he slept for a while in the sun with no more dreams.

8. RESCUE

Max was woken from sleep and dreams by barking and a horrible screeching noise not far away from him, further along the cutting. The wolf in his mind disappeared.

He stood up and peered over the top of the sandy bank. A large dog, an athletic looking boxer, was staring big-eyed and barking up into the slender branches of a sapling. Clutching one of the thin branches of the sapling, and swaying back and to in this precarious perch was the big white cat. It looked like she would fall at any second. The branches were too thin to support her weight for long, and she was clearly unused to having to grab and hold this uncomfortable position.

Although the action was taking place some tens of yards outside the boundary of his garden, Max thought he better go and investigate.

The boxer, intent as he was on his quarry in the young tree, did not notice Max approach.

"Hello mate," Max said. "Having trouble?" He stood just behind the boxer's right shoulder.

The boxer whirled round, his hackles rising. "Back off. Stay out of this. The cat's mine." He lowered his head and growled at Max.

"Doesn't look like she's anybody's at the moment," Max said.

"I can wait. Anyhow, why do you call it 'she'? Is it a friend of yours?" If dogs can summon a sarcastic tone, then this was said sarcastically in a growly whisper.

"Friend would be putting it too strong. But I know her, yes."

"Then, as I said: back off." And then after a pause the boxer added: "Cat-lover."

"I don't think I can do that, mate."

If you asked Max why he had interrupted a scene between dog and cat that goes back to time immemorial, and why he now wished to rescue the cat, or at least give it a chance to escape, he would have been hard pushed to give a good answer. Perhaps he just instinctively sided with the underdog. Even if in this case the underdog was a cat. Perhaps, if he were a Japanese bull terrier instead of an

English bull terrier, he might have said all the fuss and commotion upset his wa: his sense of harmony, especially group harmony; his serenity, calmness and well-being with the world.

But there was something else, something new. For days now a phrase the squirrel had used had stuck in his mind.

You don't always have to do what you're supposed to, the squirrel had said. Max hadn't really taken it in when Jimmy had first said it. But now for the first time he felt how right it was, and how you could use it to decide what to do in many situations, new and old.

In the situation that Max had been in, caught by his collar, never able to free himself, what a squirrel "was supposed to do" was not come to the rescue. He should have kept clear and let things, nature and fate, take their course. And if Max died, then so be it. That was fate.

But instead Jimmy had done what a squirrel wasn't supposed to do. He had saved Max's life. Max was beginning to realise the full power of the squirrel's way of looking at the world.

With this new way of looking at the world gently sparking and criss-crossing his mind, Max stood his ground and looked at the boxer with the cool eye of a professional fighter.

The long-legged brown dog was big and muscular. No doubt fast on his feet. Those were minus points from Max's perspective. On the other hand he was young and excitable and inexperienced. Those were plus points. His mouth and jaw were odd too: they might be good for hanging on with that under-bite, but probably hopeless for ripping and slashing; and not so good for protecting his neck from an attack from below. His legs too were a bit long for a fighter. Good for chasing, running down and catching small prey from behind, but not so good for providing a platform from which to launch an attack. Nor for defending against an attack for that matter. And underneath the bravado Max sensed that for all his muscle and speed his heart might not be in a hard set-to, especially if it lasted longer than a few seconds.

Max moved effortlessly into one of his well-used routines, which was to talk as though Max wasn't really up for a ding-dong battle, and then suddenly attack when the opponent least expected it. And all the while as Max talked the boxer did not notice that

Max's ears, normally held erect and alert above his head, had now dropped and were flattened flush against his skull and at the same time his eyes had narrowed to little slits set deep in their protective sockets. Like a knight in armour from the Middle Ages long ago, Max was tooling up for a fight.

Max was asking the boxer if he came there often, and where did he live, and how come they'd not met before. And then just as the boxer began to reply and say "Forget all that. Get off. This is my lan-," Max attacked.

Coming in low and hard he dodged the boxer's head and came up viciously with his jaws apart, taking a deep grip on the boxer's neck from the underside. He anchored his front toes into the earth and pulled the boxer to the ground on its side, where it thrashed and wriggled desperately.

"Another mill tighter with my teeth and you're a dead dog, mate," Max whispered through his clenched teeth. "I recommend you keep still." The boxer did as he was bid.

Still keeping his grip, Max glanced up into the tree and growled to the cat "Get going while you can." Della needed no second telling. She clawed and shuffled rapidly down from the tree and sped into the bushes above the cutting, heading for home.

"Now," Max hissed. "She's gone, mate. So give over. Let's move on to phase two. I'm willing to release my grip if you're prepared to call it a day yourself. What do you say?" He whispered.

After a moment or two's hesitation the boxer said "All right. Let go. Get off," his voice barely audible through his constricted throat, and unable to keep both the fear and relief out of his voice.

Max got in position to jump away and assume his fighting platform as soon as he released the other dog. Then he let him go.

The boxer jumped up with a snarl, a few drops of blood dotting his throat. Max could see he was briefly considering restarting the fight, maybe under the delusion that Max had been lucky or had tricked him in some way. Max took up his attack position, all four legs flexed, his ears flat, his eyes thin narrow gleams, and his head held low with his long snout angled down, protecting his neck.

"Give over," he growled. "Give it up mate. You're a big dog and you're fast, but you don't have the guts for this. But I do."

The boxer snarled "I'll get you. You won't be so lucky next time." Then he turned and bounded back through the trees above that part of the cutting, growling aggressively over his shoulder.

Max watched him go. Then called out after him: "You don't always have to do what you're supposed to," he said. "It's important. Remember it." But he didn't think the boxer would.

Then, satisfied the boxer wasn't going to change his mind and attempt to run Max down from behind, he cocked his leg and marked the narrow trunk of the sapling with a splash of urine; then turned round and made his way back to the sandy dell. "Ho hum," he said to himself. But then as always after a fight, he felt like singing. "Tirra lirra, along the railway," sang the bull terrier.

Neither dog knew it, but there was a witness to the fight. Hiding that day during daylight hours under the long grass and a thick set of brambles, Luca the fox watched the action along the railway cutting and saw the two dogs having the set-to. He was astonished at the aggression and power of the smaller dog. Yet he wasn't too troubled on behalf of the larger dog. That one had given Luca a lot of grief every now and then, chasing him up and down the line until Luca managed to give him the slip.

9. TRICKS

There are safe places to live, and some not-so safe, if you are a wild animal trying to make your way in a world run, controlled and occupied, and often laid waste and devastated, by humans. Often the best home, because less travelled by humans, is along a railway line, if you can find one. For squirrels trees are good in general, but some trees are better than others. And the best ones are taken by the most dominant squirrels. There, high up in - preferably - deciduous trees the squirrels build their home and nest, their drey.

In the neighbourhood of Max's garden the best squirrel homes in the beeches, oaks, chestnuts, cedars and silver birches were taken by the dominant squirrel families. For youngsters like Jimmy and Jenny their home had to be found among the slender saplings along the railway line. As both squirrels were still too young to breed and start families of their own, the railway line was for now as good a place to live as it gets.

As long as you were careful, and kept your wits about you, there was plenty of food around in spring, summer and autumn. And you could roam anywhere in the neighbourhood to find it. For winter you created a store by burying as many nuts as you could during the autumn, and then committed these burying places to memory.

Some humans in this area even put out pieces of bread and cheese and leftover scraps of food in their gardens. They called it "feeding the birds"; never "feeding the squirrels," though most either had no idea that much of these leavings was in fact taken by squirrels; or if they did know, didn't care as long as it didn't stay too long on their lawns and made a mess. Others did care though, very much. And they devised all sorts of means, and went to enormous lengths, to ensure the food they left was eaten by birds and none of it by squirrels.

They went to specialist shops called garden centres to buy fantastical designed apparatus that were intended to be "squirrel-proof". Some humans even redesigned and modified these pieces of equipment themselves, or came up with original designs of their own in garages or garden sheds and workshops. All to prevent squirrels eating the food that was left for the birds.

And none of it did any good at all.

There were fancy one-way cages with trapdoors and spring-loaded barriers that were supposedly squirrel-proof. There were slippery metal poles that were supposedly squirrel-proof; at the top of which you could hang special supposedly squirrel-proof wire cages full of peanuts. Yummy in our tummy thought Jimmy and Jenny. There were special chemical sprays, and impregnated materials, which squirrels were said to hate and would not cross or even go near. There were squirrel-proof ropes, wires, doors, traps, tubes, cradles, springs, poles, systems, balances, boxes, and contraptions of metal and plastic contortions of all-sorts of specifically designed apparatus. There was a whole industry engaged in the business of making equipment that would prevent squirrels accessing food that was targeted for birds.

And none of it did any good at all.

None of the specially bought, specially made, contraptions and equipment did the job it was designed to do, which was to prevent squirrels accessing the food and getting away again. The squirrels were just too good at adapting to and getting round the barriers and obstacles.

Aside from the easy hazards of supposedly squirrel-proof barriers and equipment, the main danger for youngster squirrels like Jimmy and Jenny when foraging far and wide for food was to keep out of the way of larger more dominant squirrels. And cats of course, and lively springy chasy dogs like Trice. Many a time Jimmy had been chased away from a piece of cheese or a nice chestnut he was hoping to bury by a large tail-bristling adult male or dominant female. Then Jimmy would have no choice but to back away – with a certain amount of cheeky chirping and tail bristling of his own in the big squirrel's direction - and leave the morsel to be eaten or buried by the other squirrel. But if you were careful and quick, and lived on your wits, you could and would do all right.

There was one particular garden, more of an immaculate field in fact, which most of the squirrels had learnt to avoid. This was further along the railway line towards Chester, where between the villages there were farms. And on these farms, for a thousand years since the time of the early Middle Ages, there had been herds of black and white cattle that produced milk that was made into cheese. A TV gardener and devout conservationist (as he called himself) lived here in what used to be a working farm and was now a comfortably modernised farmhouse with super-efficient insulation and double- and even triple-glazed windows and underfloor central heating and a wind-generator and a herb-growing kitchen garden and outbuildings converted to sports and playrooms.

The farmhouse was surrounded by acres and acres of empty fields, in one corner of which there still lived a token small herd of milk-cows that the conservationist paid a local farmer to come and milk.

The conservationist was a television personality who produced and fronted TV programmes that told people how to live in the country and make splendid native and exotic gardens and how to make things grow. The celebrity TV gardener's name was Robin Gordon and his most famous TV programme was called "Gordon's Gardens".

And on the large immaculate shrub-shrouded lawn at the back of the farmhouse the TV gardener had set up a long and obstacle-clustered course with food at the end of it to attract squirrels. This course was designed not necessarily to prevent the squirrels reaching the food, but just to slow them up in their progress towards it. Despite the difficulties involved in reaching the food, the food tray remained a popular target for local squirrels because loaded on it was the best and most mouth-watering food around.

This was deliberate. The food tray was designed to be very attractive to squirrels. The route to it was also designed to slow the squirrels up sufficiently to make them easy targets for the man and his son Carl to be able to shoot and pick off and kill the squirrels with air-rifles.

Though, when pushed, the TV gardener would say he hated killing things, even grey squirrels, he also believed in something he called "the greater good". And it was the "greater good" that made him trap and kill and eradicate grey squirrels.

The squirrels, grey squirrels, had come to learn that many humans hated them. They didn't know why, they just knew that certain gardens and fields were dangerous and often deadly.

The grey squirrels didn't know it, but many humans hated and detested them because they blamed them for the demise and absence of the red squirrel in these parts. They called them "tree-rats" and despised them as vermin. They hated them as immigrants and newcomers. The humans hated them as newcomers in the same way that their own ancestors had been hated as newcomers by the Heavies those thousands of years ago.

In fact, there never had been red squirrels living in the gardens and fields in these parts. But many humans believed otherwise. They believed that the grey squirrels had driven the red squirrels away, had even killed them. And they believed that if the grey squirrels were eradicated then the red squirrels would come back. Such is the danger of belief. The triumph of fiction over fact in the mind of a human is a dangerous thing.

The TV gardener believed all these things. That's what made him trap and shoot and kill grey squirrels. If he sometimes failed to shoot a squirrel but trapped it instead in a bag he would beat the squirrel to death with an ash cricket stump he had modified into a strong and superbly balanced specially made club by drilling down into one end, filling the hole with 13 one-pound coins and then plugging the end again.

"It's my thirteen pounder," he would say about the modification. "All the better for giving them a good pounding," laughing at his own joke, when he showed people what he'd done, as he often did. And he despised other people when they heard about and sometimes objected to this behaviour as cruel and inhumane.

"It's normal in the country," he would say. "That's what country people do. That's the way people live in the country. You wouldn't understand." And because country people did it that made it normal, and morally sound, and therefore good and right to be imitated by people who understood the country, like him. He believed that those who objected were not country people. They might live in what they thought was the country, but they were not really country people. They didn't know country ways. They were squeamish and sentimental. He called them precious and described them witheringly as four-by-four farmers.

10. CELEBRITY

The TV gardener possessed two chocolate labrador dogs. At all times they walked permanently at his heel even when walking in the forest and Primrose Hill and other wild places. When young, if they ever moved from the TV gardener's heel they were given a severe beating. They learned fast. Behind your heel is the proper place for a dog, he would say. He also thought it of paramount importance that a dog knew who was boss, as he put it, and that they were always under control. Control and knowing who was boss was, for some reason, critically important to the conservationist.

One of the most important things the chocolate labradors had to learn from a very young age was that they must never under any circumstances jump up. The dogs didn't understand the logic of this because, after all, to them they were just being friendly and showing their humans they had nothing to fear from them. They understood very quickly that this was a crime on a par with worrying sheep, but they didn't understand why.

As a result they were very cowed dogs, weighed down by rules and regulations and orders and commands they didn't understand. They particularly failed to understand why the issue of all these orders and commands had to accompanied by so much bad temper on the part of the humans. All their life was spent worrying about transgressing one law, order, rule, regulation, command or another. So they spent their whole lives under the assumption they did most things wrong and feared reprisals for it. They lived in fear.

The TV gardener always described his chocolate labradors as "working dogs", though any observer would be hard pushed to describe what kind of actual work they did. And in fact they didn't do anything at all that could be referred to as work, just walked slowly and dispiritedly at the heel of the man who very much thought of himself as their boss and master. It was purely that the TV gardener believed that the only worthy dogs were working dogs. All other dogs were by definition non-working and unworthy and were therefore idle pampered lapdogs and pets whose existence it would be difficult for any discerning person to justify. The only type of dog worth having was a working dog, whether that meant anything in reality or not. It was the phrase alone that counted. It implied a hierarchy of dog value. Working dogs were above other dogs because they worked for a living in some way, and therefore were more honest, more justified in their existence, and more moral in some certain but indefinable way. Whereas a dog that was a just a house-dog (said with disdain and mystification by the conservationist, as though who could possibly want such a thing, plus it was not the way dogs should be treated) and a pet was right at the bottom of the dog-pile, and was without value and no more than a whim of a sentimental owner. Unworthy dogs owned by unworthy owners. He called all such owners of house-dogs, lapdogs and pets, that is, non-working dogs, Paris Hiltons.

At point-to-points, and in the country pubs he frequented, or even on the street, if introduced to their dogs by friends and acquaintances he would always ask "Is it a working dog?" Most people asked this question were completely flummoxed for a reply, and didn't really know what the question meant.

The TV gardener was therefore definitely not amused when he met a show-business acquaintance on the High Street one day, accompanied by his basset hound, and when asked this same question "Is it a working dog?" replied "Oh yes of course. He's something in the City. He's only just started out but he's already on a hundred grand a year."

Max heard the chocolate labradors barking sometimes, but not often. Whenever they did, he could tell from their voices they were nervous, terrified and deeply unhappy. Whenever he heard their sounds an image of a great white albino wolf seemed to drift into his consciousness, but he couldn't focus on it or really pin down what it was. But whenever he heard the sad labradors barking, Max's heart went out to them and he wished there was something he could do to help them.

The chocolate labradors lived short lives with the celebrity gardener; and when one died he always replaced it with another chocolate labrador, who learnt very quickly that though he was a working dog, he was very much under control, he knew who was boss, he must never jump up, he must try not to make a mess, he mustn't bark too loudly or at inappropriate times, and he must only walk at his master's heel.

The TV gardener's wife and daughter didn't care so much about control and who was boss and whether an animal worked or not. Instead they owned horses and went riding a lot. One of the deserted fields they owned was called a paddock. Their horses lived there in sheds called stables where stuff called tack was kept. The mother and daughter spent a lot of time together grooming, and mucking out and talking about horses.

The daughter did eventing with her horse, locally and nationally, and her mother was very serious about it and put her daughter through many trials. The mother intended her daughter to represent England as an eventer at various national and international horse trials, and even in the Olympics.

The mother when young had been a showjumper and an eventer too and had dreamed when she was a girl of doing well at horseshow meetings, and doing a clear round when eventing at Hickstead and even winning a medal at the Olympics. But somehow she had never had the opportunities, she felt, that were open to richer people, and her parents couldn't afford the really good horses, and she had been forced to give it up. Now she was rich she was determined that her daughter would succeed where she herself had not been allowed to succeed.

In reality she just hadn't been very good at it; got bored with it as a teenager, and quite early on had switched her attentions from horses to boys. But in her own mind there was a different story, a mythology, that now forced her daughter on a reluctant horseback road to becoming an international calibre showjumper and eventer whether she liked it or not.

The TV gardener and conservationist (he always used this word to describe himself) was concerned that his boy might be exposed at school to other ways of thinking, other squeamish and sentimental ways - sometimes described by the conservationist as wishy-washy liberal - that definitely weren't country. And he did what he could to counteract these sentimental wishy-washy influences and bring up his son in proper country ways.

Which was why from a very early age he had taught his boy to shoot.

The boy Carl, his son, didn't care so much about what was country and what wasn't country. He just liked shooting. He especially liked shooting living things.

The boy had become something of an expert on air rifles.

Most air rifles come in two calibres: point 22 of an inch and point 177 of an inch. There are others but 22 and 177 are the most common. There are arguments among purists and aficionados about which calibre is better. Some say a 177 is not powerful enough if you want to kill something. It forces the slug out at 800 feet per second, but it's a question of the stopping power of the combined weight of the pellet and its muzzle velocity and speed through the air. They say it's okay for target shooting and piercing Coke cans and empty food tins from 30 yards, but it lacks the punch of a point-two-two, which though it travels through the air slower at 600 feet per second has more kinetic energy, they say, more stopping power. A two-two is what you need for killing things.

The boy started out firing a BSA Meteor 177. Not a bad starter air rifle, but by no means state-of-the-art. He then graduated to his dad's old hand-me-down point-22 calibre Webley Mark 3, when his dad bought a newer model. The Webley Mark 3 was a top-of-the-range weapon and did the job and the boy found it good. But more and more as he learned about air rifles the more he dreamed about owning a Walther. They were the best.

The only trouble with the Walther he wanted was that the way he wanted it modified made it illegal to own in Britain. It was too powerful to own without a firearms licence.

But Carl still dreamed. Then wonder of wonders one day his dad actually came home with one. Though illegally powerful, the gun was quite readily obtainable through particular websites on the internet and even at specialist auctions. The prized Walther was a model 3000, at 4.5 mm equivalent to a British 177 calibre. The boy didn't mind that it wasn't a point-22. He was delirious that it was a Walther.

The Walther fired in a different way to other air rifles. It didn't work by means of a compressible spring cocking and releasing a relatively slow moving piston, but came with its own reservoir of compressed air. If you filled the rifle's gas reservoir from a bottle of compressed air, as used by divers say, through a special valve the gas pressure inside the diver's bottle of 300 bar could still be at 200 bar when transferred to the reservoir in the rifle. That sort of pressure was well capable of making the Walther fire its specially designed 4.5 mm pellet at a muzzle velocity of over 1200 feet per second. At those sort of pressures and muzzle velocities, the gun was of course illegal. Also, firing from compressed gas rather than a spring-driven piston made the Walther recoilless, and therefore much more accurate.

For the next few months the back garden of the TV gardener's farmhouse became deadlier to living things than the OK Corral in Tombstone when the Earp brothers and Doc Holliday were provoking the Clanton gang.

And yet after those first few months with his new gun, with its dramatic effect on squirrels, Carl became somewhat sated and hankered after bigger game. Squirrels were good, but on his dad's obstacle course they were too easy. The boy wanted to see what effect his gun might have on bigger animals. Cats for example. Or even dogs. He thought the new gun might kill a cat, but maybe not a dog. But who knew?

Like many boys, when something is unknown and a mystery he wanted to find out the answer. He also knew that he wouldn't find these larger animals in his dad's garden. He even thought for a moment of testing the theory on one of the chocolate labradors, but rejected the idea not so much through fear of it working but more fear of being found out and held responsible if it did. He also toyed with the vision of potshotting at the small herd of milk-cows in one of the side-fields. The shots wouldn't kill them, he felt sure, but he thought the damage inflicted might be interesting. But again rejected the idea because the evidence trail would lead straight back to him. He realised he would have to go looking for cats and dogs and whatever other animals he could find further afield. He began prowling the common land along the railway line looking for suitable targets.

Even though his dad had impressed upon the boy that the new gun was illegal, and could be confiscated by the police, with a fine or even worse a custodial sentence, the boy didn't care about that.

He wanted to shoot things. And with this new gun the bigger the better.

When out foraging for food, Jimmy and Jenny had learnt from a very early age to beware the land of the TV gardener, especially his back lawn, particularly during the day despite the pull of the fresh food placed on the bird table at the end of the obstacle course. You could try your luck along the obstacle course at night, and that sometimes worked. But you had to be careful because at one point along the route a bright light would snap on illuminating the entire lawn. It was best then to immediately abandon any quest for food, jump down from the ropes, springs, wires, traps and balances of the obstacle course and run to safety in the perimeter shrubs as quickly as possible.

The squirrels didn't know it but the floodlight was triggered by a motion detector set high on the back wall of the farmhouse. It was designed that way, not to deter burglars, but to allow potshotting at night at squirrels by the TV gardener and his son, should they feel like it. As often as not they had other things to do at night, but the option was there should they wish to take it up.

Many squirrels paid with their lives in their attempts to reach the rich food at the TV gardener's table. But Jimmy and Jenny didn't. They were the only squirrels who regularly beat the course, gorged on the food, and ran away before either Robin or Carl could get a good shot at them.

The secret of their success was that they worked together. One would test an obstacle while the other watched. That way they'd both learn the solution to the problem. Sometimes, aware they were being watched, one would try to attract attention while the other sneaked to the food. Other times they'd tackle the barriers and ropes together or side by side, multiplying the potential targets, but wasting precious aiming time. They also discovered that they could hide in the bushes and trees parallel to the lawn and drop safely on to the ropes accessing the food on the bird table at any point along the route. Jimmy and Jenny became so adept at getting access to the food table despite the obstacles designed to slow them down that Robin and Carl could never keep them in their sights long enough to take a good shot at them. Nomatter how much he changed and adapted the course, the two squirrels always beat it.

Time and again both Jimmy and Jenny defeated the TV gardener's best efforts at squirrel eradication. And fed themselves at his expense at the same time. Though he couldn't be absolutely certain, Robin Gordon was sure it was the same pair of squirrels that kept making successful inroads into his trove of delicious nuts and berries. And he hated them with a pure and righteous anger.

11. TURNS

Fairground man Julian "Tools" Tilly looked out of his caravan window at his collection of attractions in the yard. Everyone in the fairground business called him Tools, and he now answered to that nickname himself. He had of course originally called himself "Jules" just like anyone else named Julian. Except in Tilly's case he always spelt it "Jewels" and ensured everyone else in the orbit of his acquaintance spelled it that way too. Tools thought spelling was important. He thought it mystical in some strange way, and that it engendered a kind of special power.

Before he owned his own attractions business, Tilly had been a mend-all, repair and maintenance man and mechanic in the fairground trade. There wasn't anything he couldn't mend or repair. If you wanted something to keep running long after the date it should have given up the ghost, way after its useful lifetime, you called in Jewels Tilly. And inevitably in that line of work with that reputation, one day one wag in the business had re-christened him "Tools". And it stuck.

Now as Tools Tilly looked out at his attractions he was convinced it all wasn't good enough. He needed something new. His business – Tilly's Turns – had many of the traditional fairground attractions, such as coconut shies, rides, hoops-and-blocks, dodgems, the strongman striker where you hit a block with a mallet to push a piece of wood up a post to ring a bell, darts and air rifles shooting galleries, and so on. They were good, traditional, well-tested attractions. But Tilly wasn't happy. They all seemed a bit old-fashioned. Business on them was tailing off. In the days of Playstations, X-boxes and iPhones, who wanted a coconut shy? Not only were the traditional attractions a little, well traditional, they also seemed a bit safe and dull.

There was also the question of giving away the right kind of swag to prizewinners these days. Did people really want an ailing parasite-ridden goldfish in a small plastic bag as the reward for winning at darts or shooting or coconut-shying? Tools Tilly didn't think they did. But he had a suspicion that people still liked to bet, and to gamble, as they had from time immemorial. He thought the attractions of betting and gambling were actually becoming stronger in modern society. He began to wonder how he might introduce betting and gambling to his attractions.

Tools Tilly looked on the internet for ideas he might be able to steal. A good source for any idea is YouTube. Tilly scanned the various categories and search-links in YouTube for ideas.

And by chance following a link he came across the Carling Black Label advert from 1989.

Tools Tilly hadn't thought about that ad for years, for decades. He had of course, like everyone else, watched the famous Carling Black Label advert of 1989. He remembered all about it.

There was a series of Carling Black Label lager adverts in the 1980s, all with the tagline at the end: "I bet he drinks Carling Black Label," said by an observer after watching someone do something pretty near impossible and/or devil-may-care heroic.

In the 1989 Carling ad, a grey squirrel was seen negotiating with ease an absurdly difficult and seemingly impossible obstacle course to reach the hazel nuts on a distant bird table. The squirrel's successful advance through the obstacle course was set to the music of the well-known 1980s TV series "Mission Impossible". At the end, when the squirrel is shown munching the nuts, and stuffing them into its gob two at a time, one of two supposedly observing owls says to the other: "I bet he drinks Carling Black Label."

Now Tools Tilly watched the advert again on YouTube and a great new idea trickled into his mind like a spring of fresh cold water emerging from the desert rocks.

Tools Tilly got on his mobile and immediately contacted two of his men, Ray and Ron, itinerant workers who between fairs found whatever work they could get as unskilled labour. They were currently engaged in erecting tents and temporary stalls and making post-winter repairs at the polo ground in mid-Cheshire on the A49 road. Tilly asked Ron and Ray to be on the lookout for a pair of squirrels. Preferably young and active squirrels.

At the same time, one day at the end of winter and the beginning of spring, the TV gardener went looking for Ron and Ray for a job. He had used them before for simple repairs round his house and estate and now wanted to hire them to repair the horse stables in the paddock. He found them after a polo game at the nearby pub the Fox and Barrel enjoying a well-earned pint of Eastgate. They were available and keen to take on the extra work.

In return Ray and Ron asked him the best whereabouts for squirrels in the area. The TV gardener pointed them in the direction of the long railway cutting at the side of his land. The two men took the three-day working opportunity on reroofing the horse sheds to set a squirrel trap in the railway cutting. They either got lucky or were cleverer than they looked, because they caught Jimmy and Jenny.

There was a witness too. Hiding that day during daylight hours under a thick set of brambles, Luca the fox watched the action along the railway cutting and saw the two squirrels being caught, then released from the traps, placed in bags and taken away by the two humans.

12. COURSE

Tilly had a yard in a run-down industrial estate on the eastern side of the town. Here, in his business premises on a concrete covered patch of land between the canal and the railway line where all the equipment for all the attractions in Tilly's Turns was stored, Tools Tilly devised an obstacle course for the squirrels, based on the Carling advert, much to the watching amusement of Ron and Ray.

Firstly a rope was suspended from a hook at the nasty concrete panel wall at one side of the premises. The rope ran 40 yards across the yard to a second hook fixed to the equally nasty concrete wall on that side. Just below the second hook, Tilly attached a platform to the wall on brackets. He covered the platform with food; cheese, bread, peanuts and hazel nuts. The platform was inaccessible from below and could only be reached by dropping from the rope line above. In between the two hooks was set a series of baffles, trapdoors, polycarbonate tunnels, spring-loaded balances, one-way chicanes, jump-points over water drums, poles and obstacles. At various places along the route Tilly added wider, easier sections where he imagined one squirrel might be able to overtake the other.

At first his squirrel-run operated in two ways. Firstly two clear polycarbonate starter-boxes were set side by side at one end of the course. The doors to the boxes would be opened simultaneously and the squirrels would race each other to the food platform at the far end of the course.

The second option involved the course being set up in a different way with the food platform being placed on a pair of steps below the rope line at the exact halfway point across the yard. The two squirrels would then be released simultaneously from their traps at each end of the rope line and race each other to be the first to drop on to the food platform.

It took many hours of practice and trial and error for Tilly to decide that the arrangement with the food platform set in the middle worked best. It offered a clearer, more central target, leading to a more exciting race for the punters. It also meant he could dispense with the various overtaking places on the course.

As an added incentive, in case the squirrels decided they were bored and refused to perform, only the first squirrel to arrive at the platform was allowed to eat. The other was scooped up into a bag before joining his mate on the food platform.

Tilly knew he couldn't do this during live shows at a fair. He thought rightly that the punters would object. But he ensured it happened all the time during "training". He reckoned the squirrels wouldn't know they would both be allowed to eat on the platform when they performed during the fair. Another difference when the "act" went live was that there would only be minimal amounts of food on the platform, enough for only one squirrel. This was to ensure the squirrels went hungry and so would be willing to perform every half-hour on the hour and half-past the hour during the day of the fair. Tilly reckoned he might get sixteen and even perhaps twenty runs a day out of the squirrels.

His idea was that this latest addition to Tilly's Turns would be a big money-spinner and it was scheduled to appear before the public for the first time at Knutsford Mayday Fair. This was an age-old traditional mayday fair, held not necessarily on May 1st but on the first Saturday in May. If successful there, and Tilly saw no reason why it should not be, he would then take what he increasingly considered the premier act among all his attractions on the road to other fairs in the calendar all round the country.

With food as the incentive – in fact it was the only food they were offered or were allowed to eat – the squirrels required very little training to get the hang of what they were supposed to do in racing each other along the obstacle course. They'd already had extensive practice getting round the squirrel-proof barriers and obstacles in the gardens round their home, as well as their numerous successful forays through the TV gardener's obstacle set-up.

After many hours practising, and after Tilly had established which was the better option for the course layout, and with yet more practice on the final layout, Tools Tilly was content. He had found himself a winner all right. And so Jimmy and Jenny were finally allowed to rest. They were placed in a wire cage in the open air in Tilly's yard. A tin of water was provided for them in the cage, but no food. At night the cage was covered by an old tarpaulin, but still left out in the open. An upturned cardboard box with a hole cut in one end served as a shelter from any rain and night chills for the squirrels inside the cage.

Tilly's idea was that people would pay to watch the squirrels race along the course, performing amazing acrobatics on the way, and defeat it if they could. That spectacle alone might be worth paying the entry price for, Tilly thought. It being a race, Tools also guessed the punters would want to lay bets on which squirrel would win, and be first to arrive at the food platform.

To enable the spectators to rapidly identify which squirrel was which Tilly planned to make them wear collars: one with a light blue collar and one with a deep red collar.

In this way Jimmy and Jenny, now renamed "City" and "United", became the latest and best fairground attraction in Tools Tilly's Turns.

As soon as they realised what the whole thing was about, and even more certainly realised how what was provided on the platform was the only food they were going to get, Jimmy and Jenny took turns to ensure they both got to the food first. They disguised it, so it looked random, with one or other of them making what looked like a mistake to any human observer as they tackled the obstacle course. The course looked fiendishly difficult so it wasn't surprising that the squirrels often were baffled or made mistakes which let the other squirrel overtake or get ahead. But for the squirrels it was the best way they could think of to ensure they both had enough to eat.

It was actually Ron who noticed the squirrels seemed to chirp and cheep and squeak a bit before each contest. "Hey Tools," he said. "I'm sure these little grey rats are talking to each other!" But Tilly told him not be so incredibly stupid. He said they were just excited. They were clearly getting used to performing and might even be getting to like it.

But Ron was right. What Jimmy and Jenny were actually doing was talking to each other and deciding which one of them was going to get to the food first on that particular run.

"It's just like that system in the dangerous garden," Jenny said. "It's much much more complicated and difficult, true. But I don't think anyone's trying to kill us here."

"True," Jimmy agreed. "But we might starve to death if we

don't both get to the food table."

Using all the experience they had gained in beating the system in Robin Gordon's garden, Jimmy and Jenny now began to use all their wiles and wit and cunning and tricks to learn and understand and beat Tools Tilly's obstacle system.

Tools Tilly on the other hand couldn't believe his luck.

"You lads did well landing these two squirrels," he said to Ron and Ray. "They're a godsend. Pretty evenly matched, it seems to me. Just what the doctor ordered."

With no obvious differences in size or athletic ability between the two squirrels, a punter wouldn't be able to tell before the race which of the two squirrels was more likely to win. And Tilly knew from all the hours of practice he'd overseen that one squirrel was as likely to win a race as often as the other. They really did seem absolutely evenly matched.

And to ensure when it came to the fair that any repeat punters couldn't learn to identify any differences in winning ability between the two squirrels, every now and then out of sight of the punters Tilly would switch the red and blue collars, so City became United, and United became City. With just two weeks to go till Knutsford Fair, in his mind's eye Tilly could already see the money rolling in.

13. OVERHEAR

And so as the captive squirrels practised in Tilly's yard for their upcoming big day at Knutsford Mayday Fair, in the gardens along the railway line winter changed its ways and moved solidly into early spring. And Max pottered around his garden, investigating and finding out through his nose all that had been happening since he was last in that section of the garden.

And Max began to wonder what had happened to the two squirrels. He hadn't seen them for a few days, almost a week, and he had begun to enjoy and look forward to their almost daily conversations very much.

He looked everywhere. He searched the rhododendrons. He peered up into the silver birches. He looked for any traces of them along the top of the railway cutting. He put his nose to the ground and really concentrated on the information coming in through that sensory channel. All without success.

He noticed that when his humans put out in the garden a bag of peanuts suspended on a special supposedly squirrel-proof slippery pole, Jimmy and Jenny weren't among the squirrels racing to be first to put the effectiveness of the squirrel-proof slippery pole to the test. The strongest smell of them was by the iron fence along the top of the railway cutting. But even that was days old now. There was no fresher scent of the squirrels anywhere.

With a slight but shrill specific woof, Max called Trice for a conference at their usual meeting point, where the brick wall dividing their domains ended and a fence made of spaced-out wooden palings began. The gaps between the palings were sufficiently large for the two dogs to see each other, give each other a good nose-to-nose sniff, and pleasantly pass the time of day.

After some minutes of the kind of conversation all dogs have when they meet: what shape are you in; where've you been; what've you seen; what've you eaten; what've you chased; where've you left a marker of your presence, and most important what've you smelt recently, Max moved the conversation on.

"I'm looking for a couple of squirrels. Have you seen them?" Max said.

"Plenty. But you don't normally chase, do you? What do you want them for? Are they good to eat?" Trice said, her brown eyes smiling at her friend.

"No, they're just friends. I haven't seen them for a while. I'm getting a little concerned."

"Friends! Wow, what's come over you. Are you getting soft in your old age?"

Max was three, a year older than Trice, a fact which Trice never let him forget.

So Max explained what had happened to him and what the squirrel had done.

Trice was astonished. "I've never heard anything like that," she said. "A squirrel helping a dog. And now a dog worried about the whereabouts of a squirrel."

But Trice promised to smell and look and ask around on her side of the property divide. Max knew that Trice didn't so much talk to other animals as try to chase them. But he couldn't think of who else he could turn to. He was at a loss.

Such was Max's urgency to see if Trice knew anything about the whereabouts of the squirrels, he took no notice of Della the big white cat, sitting silently on top of the brick wall above him, watching the world go by and cleaning her paws. But Della heard all that was said between the two dogs.

14. DEAL

Della was thinking about something she heard when she escaped from being chased up the sapling on the railway line. She'd heard the dog that rescued her call out something to the other dog. He'd said something different, something new: "You don't always have to do what you're supposed to."

It was a strange thing to say, and she kept coming back to it in her mind. She couldn't leave it alone. She knew that if she behaved like a cat then the way of the cat would look after her, as it had for her kind for always and always. And if she ever veered from that then life would be unpredictable. It could also be dangerous. And yet there was something inescapably attractive and interesting about the concept of not always behaving like a cat.

The idea seemed to open up a doorway in her mind. A doorway that led to strange and wonderful possibilities. What happened if you didn't do what you were supposed to?

And so Della too, like the squirrel and the dog before her, began a course of action that led to strange and wonderful and dangerous possibilities.

Della knew that some nights in most weeks in spring and summer a fox passed through the gardens in her orbit. Luca the fox. He had a series of food sources he would check out. The big black plastic bags put out by the large family where Trice the border collie lived, they could be particularly worthy of investigation.

Luca was in two minds about wheelie bins. Inaccessible to foxes in themselves, and therefore hateful, they were nevertheless of large but limited size. And Luca had noticed that there seemed to be an allocation of only one of these new wheelie bins to each household. And so the larger families such as that at the dog Trice's house had to augment the limited capacity of the wheelie bins by other means, especially and most commonly by putting the overspill into black bags.

And so once a week, on a Tuesday night, Luca would make his way along the railway line, up the steep bank into Max's territory, across Max's territory, into the deep rhododendron bushes, and up and over the high brick wall into Trice's garden. There silently as

Trice slept he would rip open the black plastic bags with his small sharp teeth and feast on the leftover scraps of peelings and pizzas and McDonald's and strands of spaghetti and much else besides.

And often and unjustly Trice would be blamed for the mess in the morning. Injustice is the lot of domestic animals, and Trice accepted the blame and held no grudge other than a slight and temporary dimming of her gleaming large brown eyes during the angry shouting and finger-wagging chastisement.

On most Tuesday nights Della would watch Luca as he passed. Sitting utterly still and silent on top of the garden wall, she would watch the red shadow of the fox emerge from the bushes and climb the wall and slip down like a ghost on the other side. Sometimes he would nod politely in Della's direction, as one night prowler to another, as one ghost in the night to another; for if you were a fox it never did to upset other animals if you could help it. Keep everyone onside, and there'd be plenty to go round. Live and let live and there'd be plenty for everyone was Luca's motto. And normally Della would ignore him completely.

But not this time. It was a Tuesday, the day after Della had heard Max and Trice talking about the missing squirrels.

"O Fox," she whispered as Luca slid up the wall and nodded at her as he prepared to glide down the other side. As with the time when Max spoke with Della, strange animals tend to use the Old Common Speech at first when they first address each other. It's considered polite and necessary in terms of animal etiquette. But generally, after the introductions have been made, it is considered normal for both animals to drop into the vernacular normal everyday speech, if they so wish.

Astonished at being spoken to, Luca jerked his head back in her direction and nearly lost his footing on top of the wall.

"Yer what?" he hissed, in normal speech, forgetting in his surprise the etiquette of initial animal conversation.

"O Fox," Della repeated. "Stop a while if you will. I'd like to talk to you."

All animals know there is a huge divide between what they call "fenced" animals and the others that are considered "unfenced", the free ones, those that are truly wild and are not circumscribed by houses and sheds and walls and fences and the rules of humans. Max was very much a fenced animal, and knew it. Jimmy and Jenny were very much free and unfenced, and knew it. But there is also a category in-between that has no name. Cats are very much in that category and are neither fenced nor unfenced, not free but free, and know it.

Della knew much more about the world beyond his garden than Max did. She also knew much more about the truly free and unfenced animals that came prowling and raiding through these gardens at night. And she knew that some of these animals were very well-travelled indeed and might know a lot more about the wider world around than even she did herself.

That was why she waited silently on top of the brick wall that Tuesday night for the fox to pass by.

Recovering his poise, the fox shimmered along the top of the brick wall towards the strange yet familiar cat.

"Hello O Fox. My name is Della. I'm a cat."

"I can see that love. What d'you want? I'm in a bit of a hurry."

"Not being so rude might be a start."

Luca hadn't survived all the years he had in these parts without making deals and listening to others who might have the potential to make deals. With any number of farmers around armed with shotguns who shot foxes on sight; as well as the numerous fox-hunts of the area, who, though now fox-hunting was illegal, hunted every Saturday or Sunday with total impunity, it was for foxes a dangerous neck of the woods. Luca knew all that. And he hadn't survived as long as he had without making as many deals with other animals as he could. "You scratch my back, and I'll scratch yours," he would say, another of his by-words. So now he wondered what the cat wanted and whether some kind of mutually beneficial deal might be in the offing. So he rethought his position.

"I'm sorry O Cat. My name is Luca. I'm a fox," he said politely.

The formal niceties over, the two animals could now drop into normal speech.

"I'd like to ask a favour," Della said.

"From me? A favour? I don't do favours, love."

"Well let me put it another way. I'd like to come to some kind of arrangement with you. I'd like to make a deal."

"Now you're talking," Luca said. He relaxed and sat on his haunches facing the cat.

"You know this area well, don't you"

"I get around," Luca said, very much wondering what this was all about.

"Well, I have an acquaintance. A dog," Della said.

"You're acquainted with a dog?" Luca was incredulous. "Blimey love. Other than it biting your backside I'm not sure how acquainted with a dog a cat can be?"

"Be that as it may," Della said patiently with considerable distaste at the image the fox had presented. "This particular dog needs help, and with your assistance, I'd like to see what I can do to provide it."

Luca looked long and hard at the cat. She seemed to be serious.

"All right," the fox said hesitantly. "Seems a rum do, though. Very rum."

"We're looking for a couple of squirrels," Della said.

"We? That's you and the dog? Stone me. Talk about unusual bedfellows. And talk about needles in a haystack," Luca replied. "In fact, more like straws in a haystack!" And then the fox had a further thought. "Wait a minute, love. Which dog are we talking about here?" He indicated the area below and around the wall, "Not the one I'm thinking of, surely?"

"Yes. That one," Della said coolly, gratified in a way at the new tone of respect in the fox's voice.

"Cripes, love. He's a right bruiser. Nobody messes with him."

The cat shrugged as though having such powerful friends was normal for her, and began to lick a paw.

Cats acquainted with dogs! Cats friends with the notorious hardcase dog too! And now cats and dogs looking for lost squirrels! This was bizarre indeed. Luca had heard and seen some strange things in his adventurous life, but this was right out at the furthest edge. And then he remembered the recent scene down the railway cutting. The dogfight. And, hold on, hadn't there been a large white cat stuck up a tree which had managed to sneak off while the dogs were fighting? Things became a little clearer in Luca's mind. Aha, he thought, I get it. A deal's been done here. And then, thinking about that time in the railway cutting, another thought struck him.

"Funnily enough, love, I saw a couple of squirrels being trapped and bagged and manhandled away by a couple of humans just the other day."

"You did? Where was that?"

"Just back over there," he directed his head to where the railway line ran along the bottom of the garden. "Along the line a way."

"That's very interesting," Della said. She had a feeling the squirrels in question lived somewhere along the railway. "You didn't happen to notice where the humans went, or what direction they went in?"

"No I didn't," Luca replied. Then added cautiously, "But maybe I could find out. But what's in it for me?"

"You like mice, I believe?" Della said.

"I'm known to be partial to the odd mouse," Luca said, and thought especially in winter when food was harder to come by.

"You might like them, but I'm willing to bet you don't find it easy to catch them? Am I right?"

"Maybe. But I'm not admitting anything," Luca said cautiously. He wondered where this was going.

"I on the other hand find it ridiculously easy to catch mice," Della said.

Della offered to leave mice and other dead rodents out on the top of the wall for Luca on a Tuesday night, especially in winter when food was scarcer. Luca had a feeling his bag-slashing freebie food days may be numbered anyway and leaped at such a generous offer. He thought about it, but couldn't see a catch.

"All right," he said. "You've got a deal. I'll ask around about these squirrels. And maybe you might be able to get your mate the bruiser to do something for me as well? That would be nice."

"We'll have to see about that. But anyway, how are you going to find out where the squirrels were taken?"

"You leave that to me love." Luca had certain private sources of information that he would keep to himself. You never knew when they might come in handy. He turned and made to slip down the wall into Trice's garden.

"I'll ask around. Meet again next Tuesday. Same time. Same place," he called over his shoulder; and was gone.

15. FOUND

Luca thought about the task the big white cat had asked him to do as his part of the deal. He wasn't sure he could do anything specific, but in his travels he'd definitely keep his eyes and ears open, and if he happened across any captive squirrels he'd let the cat know.

The day after he spoke with Della, Luca decided he'd go east that night in his search for food. He'd spent a large part of the winter on the western side of the town, among the farms, and even in the large forest in that part of the county. But now with spring he felt it was time again to explore the food supplies further east.

He set off at dusk, heading east along the railway line. He jogged along in the space between the oily smelly gravelly stones and the grassy banks, hiding under brambles or in the long grass when trains came by. His jog was effortless and consumed minimal amounts of energy, yet covered the ground quickly. He stopped to drink occasionally from puddles or from the various abandoned rainwater filled receptacles that were plentiful along this railway. He also stopped from time to time to investigate sounds and smells; sometimes to check out the possibility of food now; and sometimes merely to add to his mental map the whereabouts of the possibility of food for a future occasion. He found a hen coop backing on to the railway line that he hadn't seen before. It didn't look particularly secure either. He filed the information away in his brain.

Luca was constantly updating and expanding his geographical knowledge of both where food might be obtained, now and in the future, and of the locations of any inherent lurking dangers. Apart from these minor side investigations, he set a relentless mile-eating pace, passing almost silently like a shadow in the night.

But fast and silent and careful as he was, there was nothing he could do about his scent. And inevitably dogs caught a whiff of him as he passed. A racket of outraged barking would ensue, often silenced by equally outraged shouting from a human.

Dogs and their noses, Luca thought. What devil designed that nasty trick? What godforsaken animal that has its food provided for it every day needs a nose that ludicrously sensitive? For foxes that was another factor that definitely added up to making life decidedly unfair.

Luca's passage along the line was peppered by barking dogs, but apart from that there were only a couple of other incidents. He nodded once or twice to cats he passed, going about business of their own, and once had to cross the line and make a short detour on the other side to avoid a badger family working on their home sett dug into the bank of a section of railway cutting. You didn't tangle with badgers. Unpredictable and dangerous at the best of times, Luca thought. And when they had a family, well it was best they never knew you were there.

The most difficult section, where Luca felt most exposed, was along the elevated viaduct, known to the locals as "The Arches", where the railway was carried across a broad valley above the town close to the point where a smaller river joined a larger one. Indeed, until Luca had nerved himself up to venture into and across the Arches, the whole of the eastern parts of the railway line, and the open fields east of the town, had been closed to him. To by-pass the Arches, he thought of leaving the line, his food artery as he imagined it, and trying to get round the town across the fields to the north or south. He'd had a look on a couple of expeditions, but found there were too many roads to cross, and they could be very dangerous. Even the tiny ones were busy these days. In the end he felt he had no choice but to attempt the crossing of the Arches. He chose a light clear night under a full moon on the principle that his night vision was better than anyone else's and he would see danger coming, and make himself scarce, before danger saw him.

The Arches was a series of 47 industrially blackened sand-stone arches, topped with two lines of open iron fencing, and two wrought iron closed-sided girder bridges stepping across the river valley for about seven hundred yards. The line itself looked much the same as it did everywhere throughout its length, steel lines and concrete sleepers bedded deeply into ballast made of stained and greasy limestone gravel. There was a gap on each side between the built-up limestone bed carrying the metal rails and the fenced side limits of the arches. Here moss had grown in the thin ashy earth that had built up over the hundred and fifty years since the structure was built. Stunted shrubs strained to grow out of the thin detritus on the ground.

It was a formidable structure and a horrible barrier for a fox to cross.

Luca crosses the Arches

The problem was one of options, Luca knew, or more exactly, the lack of options. In any situation in which a fox might find himself, he needed options, particularly escape and getaway options. And the problem with the 700 yards of the Arches, the only option available once you were on them was to go forward or to go back. Dropping off the sides was out of the question. And once on the Arches there was nowhere to hide. Of course, the problem was purely a mental one – the feeling, when one's options were reduced, of being trapped, and of therefore the inevitability of capture or death - as Luca would be the first to admit. But that didn't make it any easier to solve.

In essence it was a problem of length. The Arches were so long. Luca was familiar with the many bridges (and the few tunnels) along this railway line, which all presented this same problem – the danger of being cornered with no escape and nowhere to hide – but the bridges were all short and could be crossed in a few seconds. The Arches was different. Even at full speed it would take minutes to cross the Arches. And that feeling of being exposed to the possibility of being cornered was the worst feeling a fox could feel. And to have that feeling for minutes on end was not something you did willingly.

It took many weeks and months when Luca was young before he felt able to attempt the crossing of the Arches. He was first establishing his own mental map by exploring the geographical area around for himself, instead of relying on his ma and da. He never let on to anyone, but he'd actually failed on his first two attempts. It just didn't feel right. And the feeling of not-rightness built up and increased the further he ventured across the stone arches. It seemed to him that the structure might even be alive, with its great stumpy legs looping and striding heavily across the valley. There was a snake-like quality to it. It was alive and it was malevolent. It was hungry and it didn't like foxes.

He even gave up the second time when he had gone further than halfway across. It was all very well claiming that to go back now was actually to travel further than to go on, but the route ahead was always full of unknowns, while the distance he had already come was known and familiar. So he'd turned back that time too.

On the third attempt he made it. And having conquered it he realised that the fear he had felt was more imaginary than actual.

In fact he found that once he ventured onto it, and became more familiar with it Luca found there was actually no or little danger. It was well away from houses and there were no people there at all. It was just that it felt strange and confined and he never did fully shake off the feeling that somehow the Arches was some kind of huge and hostile and dangerously alive serpentine foe from the age of monsters.

And above all it still felt very alien, very human. But he was used to it now, he'd conquered the dragon in his mind. It felt dead and defeated. And now he sped across the Arches like a faint red arrow.

After crossing the Arches, Luca carried on along the line. He was making for an area on the eastern side of the town, which began very soon after the line passed through the town station. Here were rows and rows of redbrick slate-roofed houses clustered round the station, in long terraces punctuated by dark entries and rear access lanes known as backs.

Further east of this area the houses stopped and the badlands began. Historically this had been the industrial area. Like many English towns this town had its industrial zone on the eastern side and its well-to-do upmarket residential zone on the western side. This was because England's weather patterns and prevailing westerly winds kept the upwind west side of any town free from the nasty smoke and smells being created on the east side.

In the fractured land on the town's eastern fringe there had once been a large ICI chemical works making use of the vast reserves of salt, sodium chloride NaCl, laid down in two thick beds below the town. Now the works were much diminished, depleted and derelict in parts. A canal steered its way in to the area from the north. In the heyday of the chemical works barges brought in supplies and took away finished chemical products. The railway passed right through the centre of the industrial zone and it too had once been busy with goods wagons and tankers and chemical containers. When the passenger trains had run through their timetables and stopped for the day, the sound of the goods wagons clumping over the points and joints in the rails throughout the night had punctuated the sleep of nearby residents for generations.

As the heavy chemical industry declined much of the land was given over to cheap-rent industrial estates. Later in other parts of the country these would be come to be known as business parks, and even office parks, but here in this town in the badlands between the railway and the canal in the shadow of the giant degenerating chimneys, towers and gantries of the chemical works they were still known as industrial estates.

It was here that Tools Tilly had established his business. Tilly's yard was set off from the road, back against the railway line, next to a fish and chip shop on one side and a tyre retread business on the other.

Demand creates supply. So grubby greasy cafes, food joints and sandwich shops and kiosks grew up among the crinkly tin sheds, wooden huts and concrete yards to serve the workforce. These food outlets created a lot of leftovers and rubbish. This rubbish was often Luca's target. Luca was a bandit for leftovers.

He was heading for a cluster of food shops serving the car showrooms and the industrial estates spread along both sides of the main road through the area. Some backed on to the railway line, while others were on the far side of the road backing on to the canal.

He left the railway line and investigated the food shops in turn. He had no luck in the backyard of the first place he came to, a breakfast café ("Nobody does a bacon butty better" said a poster in the window); nor at the pizza place nearby; nor at the curry house and the kebab joint side by side on the other side of the road. All the rubbish bin lids were closed down tight. He returned to the railway line and carried on.

Luca came silently along the track, not far from the canal. At a point he recognised from frequent visits, he stopped and turned to his left off the line. A fence made of stacked concrete slabs which slotted into grooves on two-metre high posts marked the boundary of the backyard of a fish and chip shop. Luca swarmed up the concrete wall, his sensitive pads and delicate claws gaining purchase in the horizontal joints between the slabs. He dropped down into the dark and silent backyard beyond.

He found just what he was hoping for. A large heavy thick plastic four-wheeled refuse container stood against the back wall of the shop. Normally such a rubbish container would be inaccessible to Luca. But this time someone had forgotten to put down the lid. There was a feast in prospect. He scaled the side of the bin and dropped down inside among the scraps and the easily slashable bags.

After a while Luca became aware of the sound of barking. It had been going on for some time but Luca had sensed it wasn't directed at him and had ignored it.

But now there was a particular tone to the barking that drew Luca's attention. He avoided dogs as much as he could. But he was very familiar with all the sounds that dogs made. Know your enemy was another favourite maxim of Luca's. And particularly know your enemies' noises. And there was something in the tone of this particular bark that stopped Luca from continuing to delve in the rubbish bin and made him lift his head and concentrate on the sound. This wasn't a common barking to warn off a trespasser; or even the more plaintive bark designed to draw human attention. This was a dominant bullying bark. This bark said shut up and stop your noise or you'll regret it. If you don't shut up I'll come and get you, it said. It was the kind of bark a big dog might use to a much smaller dog. Or to a much smaller animal. A much smaller animal, maybe, such as a squirrel.

The barking was muffled but was definitely coming from the other side of the concrete wall, the next premises along the railway.

Luca jumped out of the bin. He scaled the concrete wall and perched for a moment on the top, looking down into Tilly's yard. The barks were quietening down now, but still carried that bullying tone. The yard fell silent.

The yard was large, perhaps 40 yards wide by 60 yards long. There were various 40-foot steel containers in it, and a group of wooden huts and offices along the far side from where Luca perched, together with a single brick-built outhouse.

Over on the left by the double steel gates which allowed access to the road, and which were now closed, chained and padlocked, were two large wooden kennels.

Luca could see a rope running from a ring set in the concrete wall to inside one of the kennels and a long chain running from the same ring to the other kennel.

A series of ropes and tubes, wires and wheels, planks and pulleys, trays and traps, baffles and balances, all suspended in the air, stretched in a line across the yard from one wall to the other. Luca could make so sense of it, but he mistrusted it.

Luca finds the squirrels

Over on the right by the concrete wall backing on to the railway line there was something else. It seemed to be a large cage partially covered by a tatty tarpaulin.

Luca dropped down again from the wall into the backyard of the chipshop. He went up and over the other wall between the chipshop and the railway. On silent feet he glided along the railway line for about thirty yards or so, with Tilly's boundary wall on his left. He climbed the wall.

His guess about the distance had been absolutely spot on. He was right above the cage, or whatever it was.

He lay as low as he could, perched again on top of the concrete slab wall. He lay absolutely still and absolutely silent. He held his breath and concentrated on the faint sounds he had detected coming from the cage below.

What he heard, he was certain, were two squirrels having a furtive whispered conversation. They were trying to be as quiet as they could. So quiet the dogs in their kennels on the far side of the yard could no longer hear them. But Luca could.

After a long minute of listening, Luca dropped down from the wall and crept away.

16. HELP

"I might have found some squirrels."

It was Tuesday night again. Della was on the wall. A dead mouse was placed on the wall top beside her. Luca jumped up on to the wall and squatted down in front of her. He noticed there was a dog in the distance, at the far end of the garden going about his nightly rounds. He explained where he'd detected the squirrels six days before. Luca described how they were caged in what seemed to be some sort of human captivity.

"You think it's them?" Della asked.

"I've no idea, love. I just stumbled across them."

"Why didn't you let me know straight away?"

"I didn't know there was any urgency," Luca replied, a little miffed at the implied criticism. "Anyway, the whole set-up looked pretty permanent to me. It didn't look like they were going any-where."

"Of course," Della said, not wanting to upset the fox. "But you think it could be them?"

"Could be. Might be. You don't see many squirrels kept by humans like that. Might not be the right ones of course."

"It's a start though, isn't it." Della said.

"Have you talked to the dog about any of this?" Luca said.

Della had to admit that she hadn't.

Luca nodded in the dog's direction. "No time like the present, then."

"I guess so."

"But if you don't mind I'll stay out of it. Make myself scarce. I'll stay back here where I can't be seen while you go off for your chat." He shrank back and down and lay on the wall. In the dark his colour blended in with the bricks. No one would know he was there.

Now that it came to it, Della was distinctly nervous about talking to the dog. Apart from the time she'd been cornered up the tree on the railway line, they hadn't talked since the dog had given her the horrible ultimatum a few weeks before. She took a deep breath and rose and walked towards the far end of the wall where she could hear the dog rummaging and snuffling around in the rhododendrons. She came to a point on the wall above where the noise was loudest.

"O Dog," she said. "I'd like to talk with you."

The noise stopped and very soon the dog's head appeared in a gap between the rhododendrons. He was looking up at her on top of the wall.

"Hello O Cat," he said formally and politely. "My name is Max. I'm a bull terrier."

"Hello O Dog. My name is Della. I'm a cat."

Taking another deep breath, Della dropped into normal speech and said: "Max I know you've been wondering what happened to your squirrel friends."

"Oh yes?" Max said. "How come you know that?"

And so Della told Max how she had overheard him talking to Trice. (She saw Max frown at that). How she had talked to the fox. ("That's interesting," Max said at that point). How she had set in motion a certain chain of events through a deal she had made with the fox. ("That's very interesting," Max said). And how now she had some news.

"We might know where the squirrels are," she said. "Some squirrels anyway."

Suddenly she had all his attention.

She explained where the fox had said they were being kept.

"I know that area," Max said. "I've been on walks along the path by the canal there quite a few times." What was more, Max thought to himself, he knew the way there too. By road.

"So they are in some kind of captivity?" Max asked. "Can you tell me again where exactly they are?"

"I think you better come and talk to a friend of mine," Della said. "Follow me."

She turned round and walked slowly along the top of the long brick wall back the way she had come. At the base of the wall, Max followed her progress, pushing the bushes aside where they got in his way. Della stopped at the point where she had just recently been talking with Luca. She couldn't see him, but she thought he was still there. The mouse she had caught and killed was gone.

"Luca," she called. "Come out and talk please. You'll be perfectly safe up here."

Nothing happened for a long moment. Della thought perhaps the fox would not emerge, that his innate caution would prevent him coming out brazenly into the open to talk to a dog. But then a shadow a few feet away seemed to move, and then Luca was there, standing low on his tensed legs, ready to spring away at the first hint of trouble or danger.

"Had me in two minds there, love," he said. Then he looked down at the dog below.

"Hello O Dog. My name is Luca. I'm a fox."

The dog looked up at the two shapes perched on top of what he always thought of as his wall.

"Hello O Fox. My name is Max. I'm a bull terrier."

There was a silence as the dog and the fox gauged each other. Max broke the silence: "Thanks Luca for what you've done."

Luca was about to reply flippantly with something like 'all in a day's work'; but then thought better of it and reverted to his truer type: "Maybe you can do something for me sometime, feller."

"I'll look into it. But first, what can you tell me about the squirrels?"

The fox explained the situation the squirrels were in, where they were, how he'd found them purely by chance on one of his food forays. "It was just blind luck," the fox admitted. "It didn't need any great expertise on my part."

Max gathered all he could from the fox about where the yard was ("I'm pretty sure I know that place. I've seen it on a sniff-around with my humans, what they call a walk," he said as Luca described it). And about the kennels and the guard dogs ("Chained up? That's good," he said). And the large cage the squirrels were kept in ("Mm, that's not so good").

"And that's about it," Luca said. "There's a pair of squirrels being kept in a cage in a large yard somewhere the other side of town." He nodded slightly with his head towards the town.

"Any clues as to what it's all about?" Max asked.

"No idea, feller." Luca said. Luca had long before decided that what humans got up to often defied all understanding. He did describe the strange aerial system of ropes and apparatus that crossed the yard.

"Some kind of alarm system or trap d'you think?"

"Again, no idea."

When he'd learned all he could of what the fox had found out, Max thanked him and the cat.

"For what you've done, Luca, unasked by me, I'll never bark at you or cry a warning to others should I ever see you," Max said. "You will always have my silence. You've given me a lot to think about."

The animals parted politely and went their ways in the night.

17. LOST

Max spent a sleepless night. He was thinking hard. He was beginning to feel an urge to investigate. This is a very powerful instinct for a dog; almost irresistible. He put it no stronger than that for the moment: investigation. Maybe he'd go and see, and see what he could see. And when he got there if he found he could do something about the squirrels' captivity then all well and good. That would be a great thing. But Max knew it wouldn't pay to be too optimistic. But all he could do was go and see. And if they were there at least he could say goodbye to them.

The question was, how?

He was fairly confident he knew exactly where the yard and compound was the fox had described. It wasn't the yard so much that made Max certain he knew exactly the place Luca described. It was the chip shop next door to it. He'd been taken by his humans on the walk along the canal there many times. The path went very close to the yard on the other side of the road, and he'd salivated on quite a few occasions at the smells flooding out of the chip shop next door.

He knew the route to the place where his humans left the car at the beginning of the walk. So finding the place would be no problem. It meant walking through the centre of the town, but Max knew that all he had to do was look purposeful – look as though he knew what he was doing – and all humans would generally leave him alone. They wouldn't assume he was lost and try to rescue him. He knew the walk place was something like a ten or fifteen minute drive away. He thought on foot it would take him no more than thirty minutes, forty at the most, at a run and persistent dog-trot.

The problem was still, how?

The how in particular was how could he get away from his home and his humans without them worrying? He knew his humans thought their house and garden were properly fenced in (except along the railway line) so that Max wouldn't stray on to the road. But Max's humans didn't know that Max could easily scramble up and over the fence any time he wanted to. He just never did it because he knew his humans didn't want him to.

As he turned and turned on his bed in the kitchen the solution came to him.

Through most of the year Max slept indoors on a bed in the kitchen. In the summer months he also had the option of sleeping out on a separate bed on the roofed but otherwise open porch in front of the kitchen door. If he wanted to. He would be let out every night to make his rounds when his humans got ready for bed. In summer if it was warm, and he fancied it, he wouldn't return after fifteen minutes or so to the kitchen door to be let back in. He would remain in the garden longer. Max's humans took that as a sign he wanted to sleep out that night on his bed on the porch. They locked the door and went to bed, leaving Max outside. This happened quite frequently during the summer.

It never happened during winter nor in the quite chilly nights of spring. Yet the more he thought about it, the more he thought it would work now too. At least he could try it and see what happened.

That night Max's humans let him out as usual. He made his rounds. Then he did not return to the kitchen door. Instead he hid in the rhododendrons and watched. After twenty minutes or so one of his humans appeared at the kitchen door, whistled and called his name. Max ignored it. After five more minutes the human disappeared inside and returned carrying a dog bed which the human set down in the porch. Then the human closed the door again. Max heard the key turn in the lock. Shortly afterwards the house was dark.

Max waited another half hour. It was around half-past midnight. There had been a flurry of traffic some time before as the pubs closed, but now the road on which the house stood was quiet.

Max emerged from the bushes and crossed the lawn to the fence on the side of the garden where a gravel drive headed towards the road. He broke into a run and scrambled up the wooden paling fence and dropped down the other side. He trotted up the drive and stood under the yellow street lights looking down the road to the town.

Back on the brick wall on the other side of Max's garden, Della the cat watched all the action. What's he doing? She thought.

Where on earth is he going? Is he running away?

Leaving home is always hard for a dog. Finding home is easy: a dog can often smell their way home from many miles away. But leaving home is always a wrench. Though dogs have a powerful urge to investigate, and will often wander far from home, they do it with a strong sense of awareness that the wandering life is hazardous and it may turn out that they might not see their home again.

Max felt that pang now. He turned and looked back at his home. He tilted his nose up and took a long strong smell of his home. Then he set his mind, took a deep breath and turned away and began to trot down the pavement by the side of the road towards the town.

First it was houses on both sides of the road, set behind privet and holly hedges and wooden panel fencing, and the occasional low brick wall. Some with gates, some without. Then came a section of shops: bookmakers, hairdressers, a cake shop, downmarket jeweller, a cheap booze place. Then a church set high on a hill on his right hand side as the road swooped down a steep hill towards the river valley below. Max trotted strongly on. At the bottom of the hill a river approached the road from the right and ran alongside it. The railway viaduct known as the Arches was silhouetted against the night sky to Max's right. Then ahead of him along the road he came to a steel bridge. Max's nails clicked on the steel decking of the pedestrian way across the bridge. Once over the river bridge Max was in the centre of the town. Max had a feeling he was about halfway to his destination.

Here there was a choice of routes. To the right slightly was the main road which carried the traffic past the town centre. But ahead was the old high street, now traffic-free and pedestrianised. Max took the pedestrian route. He knew that both roads merged again at the top of the town.

It was quiet. The shops shut. The pubs closed. The restaurants empty. Max pushed on, panting now. The street went uphill gently as it turned away from the river. Now the shops fell away and houses returned. Terraced houses with doorways straight on to the street. Many with red dolly-stoned steps. Two windows above; a door and one window below. Then came the station at the top of the town.

And next to it a medium-sized Tesco with a large parking area. Max ran on past the supermarket.

And after the supermarket came a large diy store on one side and a collection of car showrooms on both sides of the road. And after that lay the semi-derelict chemical works and the old rundown industrial estates. Max slowed down to a walk.

He arrived at the canalside car park on the left side of the road. He followed the old towpath on the side of the canal parallel to the road. Quite soon he began to catch old food smells in the air. Pizza. Sandwiches. Meat pies. Sausages. Gravy. Kebabs. Curry. Massala sauce. Bhajis. Sweet and sour.

Fish and chips.

He focused on the stale smell of fish and chips. His nose narrowed the smell down to a building on the other side of the road. Next to the fish and chip shop was a section of concrete panel wall and then a pair of large steel gates, set back from the road. Max left the canal and crossed over the road to take a look.

He stood on the road outside the steel gates to Tilly's yard and peered through the gaps between the rusty horizontal bars. The street lamps threw yellow light across much of the yard. It illuminated the far wall sufficient for Max's eyes, extremely sensitive to low light conditions, to see the whole of the far wall of the compound.

The wall was bare. The ground in front of the wall was bare. There was no large cage anywhere in the yard. Nor was there any sign of the strange array of ropes and tubes and planks and pitfalls that Luca had described suspended across the yard. Two kennels stood close to the gate on either side. They were empty. Max could see a rope and a chain lying abandoned halfway across the yard.

Max tilted his nose up slightly and took several short sharp breaths, testing the contents of the air. He could smell dogs and humans. The dog smell was strong, but it was not fresh and not active. The human smell was much less strong, and Max could tell there were no humans nearby. There was also another smell. He focused his nasal receptors on the faint aroma. The mucus on the outside of the end of his nose collected and concentrated the scent molecules. He got it, momentarily, then lost it again. He concentrated harder, gently nodding his head up and down, and widening and flexing his nostrils to gather in and sift more of the telltale molecules. He got it again, stronger this time. Squirrel!

It was definitely squirrel. But it was not fresh. There had been squirrels here, very recently. But they were not here now. The dog trusted his sense of smell completely and absolutely. It could not lie. It told him all he needed to know. There had been squirrels here in this yard. But they were not here now. The yard was deserted and the squirrels were gone.

Disappointed and dejected, Max turned and made his way dispiritedly back the way he had come.

18. TALK

Next morning found Max lying a little sadly in the sun at the end of the lawn next to the rhododendrons. The spring sun was gaining strength and Max was feeling tired and drowsy. A voice calling his name broke through his sleep.

"Max. Max." It was Della calling from the wall above.

Max pushed through the bushes and looked up at the white cat.

"What happened to you last night?" Della asked. "I saw you climb over the fence and disappear down the road. I thought you were running away. What's the matter?"

Max was quiet for a while and didn't reply. Both animals became aware of the silence.

"I went to see if I could find the squirrels," Max said at last. "I wanted to say goodbye to them."

"On your own!" Della was surprised.

"Er, yes. I didn't think I could ask anyone else to come. They're my friends and I'm the one that's worried about them."

"I would have come with you," Della said, a little surprised at herself. "Sometimes two is better than one," she added. But she wasn't sure if that was true.

"Would you?? I'm really grateful. But in any case, they're not there anymore. They've gone."

"Gone?"

"Yes. The whole place is deserted."

Max told the story of his adventure in the night.

"So that's it I guess. They've gone and we have no idea where. They could be anywhere now," Max said as he finished the story.

"And we've no reason to suppose they'll ever come back to that yard?" Della asked.

Max gave a dog-shrug.

"Well at least you tried," Della said. "That was an amazing thing to do. I didn't realise you knew your way around so well."

"I don't really." Max was the first to admit that his geographical knowledge was not good, limited as it was to where he'd been taken for walks or had glimpsed from a car window. "It was all just luck."

"Oh well," Della said. "Humans have got them. They're gone now."

"Yes I suppose so," Max said.

Della could hear the sadness and disappointment in his voice. It seemed part of the sadness was a feeling that by capturing and probably maltreating his friends, humans had let him down in some way.

Later that day Della ran into Luca by accident as he lay hidden under some ferns and long grass in the railway cutting. She had shadowed and tracked a vole that headed into the ferns and was much surprised to find Luca there as she stealthily ducked her head under the ferns to ambush and corner the vole.

"Ooh, you made me start. You gave me quite a shock," Della said as she joined the fox. "I didn't expect to see you under here."

"Not as much of a shock as I've just given that vole," Luca said, licking his chops. "How's it going with you love?"

"Not so good, I'm afraid." She told Luca the story of Max's expedition in the night to find the squirrels.

"Wow," Luca said. "He's keen, isn't he. And they're definitely not there?"

"No. No sign of them Max says. Gone quite recently he says."

Luca knew that dogs could gather incredible amounts of information through their nose.

"Must have gone the day after I heard them," Luca said. "Or soon after."

"Strange business."

"Isn't it. Still, I'll keep my eyes peeled. You never know."

19. SPECIALIST

For the first time in his life Luca was feeling guilty. So strange and alien to him was the emotion that for a while he didn't recognise it for what it was. The story of the missing squirrels kept coming back to him and stayed running through his mind. Their disappearance from the yard where he'd found them kept nagging him. He realised that if he'd talked to the cat sooner the dog would have had time to visit the squirrels and say goodbye to them, if that was what he wanted to do, while the squirrels were still there. And yet it wasn't just that. It wasn't just a question of wondering what had happened to them and where they'd gone, there was something else.

It took a while before Luca realised what it was. What was causing the squirrels to keep popping into his mind like some tiresome human springy toy?

Then he got it. A stab of guilt hit him. He realised he actually hadn't fulfilled his part of the deal he had made with Della. He hadn't actively looked for the squirrels at all. He'd actually done nothing. All that had happened was that he'd stumbled across them while out and about on one of his food searches. All well and good, certainly, and he'd passed their whereabouts on to the cat. She for her part was now providing mice, laid out on the wall top.

But had he Luca done enough to deserve it?

The guilt was telling him he hadn't.

And the trouble with a deal was that if you didn't fulfil your side of it, then sooner or later it would come back and bite you.

Once the guilt took its hot yet icy grip on his mind it wouldn't go away.

Luca knew he had to do something about it.

His first thought was that he could keep looking for the squirrels on his own, as he travelled far and wide in his search for food. That had worked before. And as an extra there was a jackdaw family he'd done deals with in the past; and more recently he'd made a loose food-searching and hazard-spotting arrangement with a couple of magpies. Both of those types of contact might be useful now.

But as the guilt kicked in and as the more he thought about the scale of the problem the more he thought now they might need something a bit better. Luck and general practice spies and thieves were all very well, but for this job he thought he might need to see a consultant.

He'd been incredibly lucky to find the squirrels the first time. Now the search had to be a bit more systematic. The more he thought about it, the more he reckoned this job needed the expertise of a beady-eyed specialist. And to Luca's knowledge there was nobody in the area, nobody for that matter for miles around, more beady-eyed than Barry. Luca reckoned his old mucker Barry might just be able to assist with this one.

Barry lived in a copse of beech trees near the Golden Pheasant pub not far from this same Cheshire Lines railway as it ran through Plumley station, nine miles - half a night's walk - to the west. Barry was a buzzard with unbelievably sharp, accurate and almost telescopic eyesight. If anything moved in this area, or better still if it was dead and didn't move, Barry knew about it.

Luca and Barry had met one night over a lamb carcass.

Ranging far and wide as he did in search of food, Luca the fox had a huge knowledge of the area. He knew sometimes that in the farmers' fields spread out on both sides along the railway line there would be occasionally dead sheep, and in the spring, dead lambs especially. One night ranging far along the line he spied a lamb carcass by a hawthorn hedge at the side of a field. A big brown bird was feeding on it. Luca had gone over and introduced himself.

"Share and share alike, brother," Luca said. "Plenty for everyone." And much to his surprise the big brown bird had agreed. The big bird had agreed because he too, just like the fox, didn't want to make enemies in the area if he could help it. His kind had made too many enemies in the past, to their cost.

They then went through the formal how-do-you-dos.

"Hello O flighty one," Luca had said by way of introduction. "My name is Luca and I'm a fox."

The tall brown bird with the viciously hooked beak replied: "Hello O fox. My name is Barkan. I'm a buzzard." And then because buzzards were very new to the area and felt they needed as many friends as they could get he added, "But you can call me Barry."

"I've been re-introduced," Barry added.

"What d'you mean? We've already said hello and introduced ourselves," Luca said. "We don't need to do it again."

"Not introduced. Re-introduced."

Luca and Barry

And Barry had told him the story he'd learnt from his mother, who learnt it from her mother before her, who learnt if from an aunt before her, how buzzards had been brought back into these parts.

The large brown lighter–fronted birds of prey and carrion hunters used to be fairly common in these parts, but their numbers had been drastically reduced through a number of factors. When the deadly disease myxomatosis struck the rabbit population, their main predator the buzzard declined swiftly in numbers too.

The survivors were easy prey to farmers and gamekeepers who blamed them, wrongly, for the deaths of a few lambs in the spring.

"We do take lambs," Barry told Luca one time as they were chatting over a dead rabbit which Barry had caught and was sharing with the fox. "But not that many, and never if the lamb is defended by the ewe, which most mothers tend to do. More lambs die of natural causes in the spring than we ever take. But who in their right mind is going to ignore a dead lamb when they spy one? Not me. But we got blamed for the lot. And we got shot. All of us."

And so in a phrase that would have delighted the heart of the TV gardener, the buzzards were eradicated from the area.

Another key reason the buzzards – and other raptors - had disappeared from Cheshire and much of the rest of England was the use by farmers in the 1950s and 1960s, right up to the 1970s, of the family of fertilisers known as the organo-chlorines. DDT was the most famous of these, but others included Aldrin, Endrin, Lindane and BHC (benzene hexachloride). These chemicals built up in the bodies of the prey eaten by the buzzards. In turn the chemicals built up in the bodies of the buzzards. The single most deadly effect of the chemical build up was the effect it had on buzzard eggs. It had the effect of weakening and thinning the shells of eggs so chicks did not survive to be hatched.

Buzzard numbers crashed.

But by the 1990s the organo-chlorines were banned, and over the years the rabbits began their slow but accelerating recovery from myxomatosis and their numbers exploded again. And the buzzard numbers began to bounce back as the rabbits proliferated, and with their numbers their habitats grew again too. Some buzzards came out of the west from their last remaining strongholds, following the rabbits. And others were re-introduced by ornithology clubs and societies and private estate owners in certain areas of the country.

Barry was a descendant of a small group of buzzards that had been re-introduced into the park land surrounding a large country house not far away, which also possessed a private nine-hole golf course in the grounds.

"To do something about the rabbits," as the owner put it when asked why the buzzards were brought back. "They're wrecking the greens." The buzzards had since done well and thrived and spread. The greens were doing all right now too.

And as they got to know each other, chatting at night over a dead lamb or rabbit, the fox and the buzzard hadn't so much made a deal as come to an arrangement. If in their travels by wing and foot they saw something eatable, preferably dead in Barry's case, they would pass on the information to each other when next they met.

20. DEAL

Plumley station was a heck of a long hike to go on a spring night, Luca thought, but a deal was a deal, and Luca was a fox of his word. Anyway, Barry might share a rabbit with him, or let him in on the whereabouts of a bit of nice carrion or even a dead lamb. If so he wouldn't have to make his way all the way back on the same night, he could spend the day over there resting up with a full stomach. So the long round trip might be worth it.

Luca had learnt it was quite safe to travel along the railway line even in broad daylight. It didn't even matter if trains came by, they never stopped. But you could never be too certain about the intentions of the occupants of various gardens and buildings spaced out along the line. There could be dogs loose too. So though a fox could travel in the daytime if he wished or was desperate, a wise fox always preferred to move at night. Humans tended to sleep at night. Some buildings that were full of people during the day were deserted at night. And dogs were generally either inside houses or sheds or were in other ways more controlled and curtailed at night. The night was definitely better for moving around.

Once again Luca made his way east along the track on a dark cloud-scudded night. He travelled the same route he had before. Through a country station halt; across the Arches; through the main town station; past Tilly's yard in the industrial estate east of the town in the narrow badlands between the railway and the canal; and so into open country beyond.

In the open country and farmland east of the town, where the line emerged from cuttings and ran along on high embankments across the plain, Luca left the edge of the line and descended to the base of the embankment and carried on his way there, alongside the iron and sometimes wood fencing, so as not to be standing out, clearly visible against the skyline. If you were a fox you could never be too careful. You never knew who might be watching.

He made good progress and arrived in the vicinity of Plumley station only two hours or so after he set out. In a break in the clouds, he could see the beech tree copse on its little rise ahead, behind the Golden Pheasant, its budding upper branches silhouetted against a nearly full moon in the spring sky.

Luca entered the copse and began to look around. There were telltale signs on the floor of building work above. It looked like nesting activity had been going on recently up in the high branches. He scented around on the ground, then looked up.

Suddenly without warning his instinct told him to duck. He ducked his whole body down, with his belly on the ground and his legs tensed ready to spring away. He was down just in time for a pair of razor-sharp talons to miss the back of his neck by a fraction of an inch.

He heard an urgent voice calling from higher up. "No, no. He's a friend. No. Leave him. Beryl, it's all right."

Luca saw a brown bird shape soar away into the higher parts of the beech trees. Then a more familiar brown bird shape dropped down with a flutter of decelerating wings and stood at the base of a tree in front of him.

"Sorry about that," Barry said. "Beryl was protecting the young ones."

"No problem. All in a night's work. But firstly congratulations, feller, both to you and Beryl is it?"

"Yes, Beryl and I have mated for life. In fact I think she might feel a lot happier if we carried on our conversation further afield," Barry said. "Away from the little ones." He paused then added: "Tell you what: there's a little something to eat over the side of the field there. Let's go over and have a bite and a chat."

Barry leapt into the air, and slowly flapped and soared out of the beeches into the open field nearby. Luca followed his line of flight and found his friend standing above the substantial remains of a rabbit by the field's surrounding hedge.

"Dig in," Barry said. "We've already had as much as we can eat."

Between mouthfuls, and often with a full gob, Luca told Barry why he had come.

Barry agreed he would have a good look round for the squirrels.

"We suspect they may be in captivity in some way. I agree, it's all pretty vague and hopeless. And why humans should want to capture and keep squirrels I've no idea. Maybe it's something, some game maybe, for some baby humans. We just don't know. But I said I'd help."

"You say 'we'," Barry said. "Who's 'we'?"

Luca said "Don't ask. It's a weird one. I'm not really with them, not really part of it. Just obliged to help through an arrangement I made. It's a dog and a cat."

The buzzard's round eyes widened in astonishment. "You're right. That is weird. But nomatter, a deal's a deal, so I completely understand. Anyway, I'll be glad to help out and have a recce," Barry said. "I'll be out up there looking the look anyway. It's no big deal to watch out for a couple of imprisoned squirrels as well. If they're out in the open, I'll spot them."

Barry was the only one among his contacts that Luca never had to make a direct and specific deal with. Their regular and constant and frequent exchange of information had benefited them both. And, as Barry said, it was all in a day's work for him "looking the look" as he put it.

Luca had his fill of the rabbit. He chatted a good while longer to the buzzard. Some time later, as the first glimmers of dawn seeded the eastern sky, Barry went back to his nest, and Luca found an old badger sett under the hedge he could rest up in for the following daylight hours. The next night, after more rabbit, he returned along the railway line to his patch.

Before they parted he asked Barry to get him any news as soon as he could. "I'll come over this way again if you like," Luca said.

"Best not, just at the moment," Barry said. "Better wait till the chicks are a bit bigger. I'll come over your way this time. I'll find you. Look out for me in a couple of days."

Luca put his head down and set off for home at his ground-eating pace. He thought as he went that if the squirrels could be found, Barry would find them. If Barry didn't locate them after no more than a couple of days, it would mean one of three things: the squirrels were being kept indoors; or they were no longer in this area; or they were dead. Did humans eat squirrels? Luca wasn't so sure they did. They didn't eat foxes either, but that didn't stop them killing them. Luca thought that all three of those conclusions would not be good news to tell the big white cat. Luca loped on down the railway line like a feather in the night.

21. OBSTACLES

Jimmy was getting low. He could see no end of this dreadful performance he was now part of. Escape now seemed out of the question. It was Jenny who held it all together through those awful days.

At first Jimmy thought it all wouldn't last long because it would be relatively easy to escape. It must be. After all, what human can contain a squirrel? It turned out this one could quite easily. There were a couple of problems.

The first problem was the netting.

Tools Tilly hadn't got the nickname he had without good reason. Thinking it all through in his mind's eye, he realised the essential problem if his new attraction was going to work would be how to get the squirrels to perform in a public space without giving them the opportunity to escape? And quite quickly he realised that netting would be the answer. Specifically, he thought a certain type of netting would be perfect. He thought cricket nets would be just what the doctor ordered.

He thought the mesh of a cricket net might be large enough to give good visibility through it for the punters watching the action going on behind the netting; and large enough also to make it impossible for a squirrel to climb up, down or along it. And yet the mesh was small enough not to let squirrels pass through the holes. Cricket nets would do the trick all right, Tilly thought.

He sent out Ron and Ray in the white van at night to steal some cricket nets.

"Look for a cricket club that's pretty secluded. There's a couple of clubs along the A50 towards Warrington that're pretty quiet. Check those out."

Tools had been very specific. He wasn't interested in the modern type of cricket nets, a ready-made self-contained affair of frame and nets on wheels. He wanted the old-fashioned type of netting, consisting of loose nets, green wooden posts, guy ropes and pegs. That was what he was after.

Ray and Ron struck lucky at the first hit. The first cricket club they found was set well back from the road (though its large white sightscreens were the giveaway from the road that a cricket ground was there). The ground and pavilion were deserted, yet standing by the side of the field were two types of cricket practice net. One was the modern wheeled type, which was mobile and was pushed on to the playing surface for practice. The other was the old-fashioned nets, the immobile fixed type with poles and guy-ropes. What's more, there were two sets of the old-fashioned type next to each other: one set surrounding an artificial Astroturf practice strip, and the other set surrounding a newly mown grass practice strip.

Ron and Ray couldn't believe their luck. It took no more than an hour for the two men to disassemble the nets, stow them away in the white van, and be heading back towards Tools's yard with about three hundred feet of prime cricket net.

Tools was right. The nets worked a treat.

Erected round the complete squirrel run, with plenty left over to make a netting roof too, the nets became a serious problem for any idea the squirrels had about escaping, and were the prime cause of Jimmy's chronic low spirits.

There was another problem too.

There were dogs.

Three of them. Two german shepherds and a jack russell, all belonging to Tilly. The effect of the german shepherds on the squirrels was more psychological than actual, since their primary function was to act as guard dogs. They took little interest in the squirrels. Their names were Sid and Dick.

The jack russell was something else. He was much worse than Sid and Dick. With that dog, it seemed to be personal.

The jack russell's name was Snough. It was pronounced "snuff", and Tools's acquaintances and workhands such as Ron and Ray thought it was spelt that way. But it wasn't. Tools was insistent that spelling was important. He couldn't tell you why, but he was convinced that good and accurate spelling meant something. It was spelt Snough because it was short for "That's enough." And the dog was called that because that's what Tools felt he had to keep saying to it all the time when it was a pup.

The first time Jimmy and Jenny had become aware of Snough the jack russell was early on their first day in Tilly's yard. A bouncy and incredibly energetic small brown and white dog had come up to their cage and said "Hey Deadmeat. I'm watching you. My human wants you to do certain things. I recommend you do them. If you don't you'll have to answer to me." He snarled and showed his teeth. "Get the picture?"

Jimmy did, but thought it was worth trying to talk to the dog. After all, it had worked once before.

"Hello O Dog," he began.

"Shut it," Snough the jack russell replied. "Don't talk to me Deadmeat."

And that was all he said by way of introduction. Sid and Dick the two german shepherds ignored the squirrels. Their job was protecting the yard from burglars, thieves and vandals at night, and giving Tilly, Ron and Ray advance warning of any visitors during the day.

In fact the guard dogs' prime function during the day was to give Tilly advance warning of visitors, in case they were business rivals and competitors. The earlier that Sid and Dick barked the better. The more time Tilly and his men then had of getting any sensitive equipment under cover and away from what he was certain would be prying, jealous and thieving eyes.

And now with this latest addition to Tilly's Turns, the barking dogs gave Tilly a chance to meet any visitor outside his premises, so they could see nothing going on inside at all.

The german shepherds were chained up permanently and slept at night in kennels in the yard. Snough the jack russell went everywhere Tools went and lived with him in his caravan.

Every day, gloved hands would reach into the squirrels' cage, grab the squirrels and place them in a bag each. The squirrels would emerge from the bag at each end of the obstacle run.

It was no good refusing to join in, Jenny had insisted to Jimmy.

"You just won't eat if you do that," she said. "And anyway, what do you think will happen to us if we don't perform like they want us to?" She added.

And Jimmy had to agree. There were plenty more squirrels out there for the taking. What was more, Snough the jack russell was eyeing them constantly. Constantly and hungrily.

"I'm not sure which he would prefer," Jenny said. "For us to do everything his human wants, as he says; or in reality for us to refuse, so he can eat us."

Like it or not, the squirrels were repeatedly made to run the course. Over and over again.

Tools tried the collars on for the first time. They looked rather fetching, he thought. As well as getting familiar with what they were supposed to do on his fancy obstacle course, Tools realised the squirrels also had to get used to wearing collars. He didn't want to leave anything to chance. He didn't want to let anything spoil the big day at the fair.

As soon as the collars were looped round their necks, the squirrels tried to shake them off. It took a long time, and a hot-eyed hungry stare from Snough, before they settled down and began to ignore them. Tools decided it was better to leave them on for good and not take them off at all. The final nail came when Snough sidled up to the cage and added his twopenn'orth too.

"If my human wants you to wear those collars, you better wear them," he snarled. "So stop all your shenanigans and get used to 'em sharpish."

Very soon Tools was pleased to see the squirrels stop trying to shake off the collars and wear them as if it was the most natural thing in the world.

As well as a way of identifying which was City and which was United, the blue and red collars also provided a means by which the squirrels could be scooped up and bagged when they completed the run. Tools had designed and made a couple of special hooks on long poles for this.

By the time that Knutsford fair was only four days away, Tools was pretty sure he'd thought of everything and it was all going to work as he intended.

The first that Jimmy and Jenny realised something new was about to happen was when all the painstakingly erected squirrel run, nets and protective screen began to be dismantled. The one bonus as far as they were concerned was that they weren't required to run the obstacle course for the whole of that day.

That day the whole of the entire squirrel run attraction of forty yards of obstacles, nets and surrounding screens was dismantled, numbered sequentially, and packed into Tilly's wagons and containers along with all the other tried and tested fairground attractions that Tools Tilly had created or stolen or brought together in various ways over the years.

Tools Tilly decided he would take the show to the fairground on Knutsford Heath two days earlier than normal to erect the squirrel run. This involved not just putting up the netting around it; but also creating a kind of closed arena with plywood screens and panels on 4x2 timber frames, plus a couple of the forty-foot containers in which the attractions were stored and transported, around the whole affair. This was Tools's way of ensuring that no punter could see the attraction without paying to get in.

He'd also had a batch of special posters printed announcing the new attraction. The posters showed a couple of cartoonish squirrels, one wearing a bright blue collar, the other a bright red one. "The Great Squirrel Race" it said on all the posters at the top. In one the squirrels faced up to each other wearing huge boxing gloves. In another the two red and blue collared squirrels raced each other side by side on BMX bikes. In a third the squirrels lined up at a sprint-line under starter's orders – a cartoon version of Tools himself holding a starter-pistol in the air.

The words on the posters underneath the cartoon image were always the same. They said: "Watch City And United In The Great Squirrel Race." And "Will City EVER Beat United? OR Will United ALWAYS Beat City?" The posters would be pasted all along the outside of the wood and container screens surrounding the squirrel-run arena.

Once everything was built, in those two days before the fair began, for the squirrels it would be practice, practice, practice.

And then during the day of the fair, as well as paying to get in, he would have Ray and Ron and a couple of other hired hands moving through the crowd laying, and taking, bets on whether City would beat United to the food, or whether it would be the other way round. Tools himself would act as master of ceremonies, commenting on the action through a microphone.

The convoy of lorries, containers, vans and caravans that made up Tilly's Turns made its way to Knutsford Heath. The vehicles arrived at their designated area and men and women rapidly poured out of them and immediately set to work.

For the second time in two days Jimmy and Jenny squirrel were not required to run the gauntlet of the obstacle course that day. And for the second time in consecutive days they were given food inside their cage. For the rest of the time they watched from their cage as Tilly's grand design began to take shape over the course of that long day.

At the kind of temporary work-camp they had established on Knutsford Heath, there was nowhere indoors to stow the squirrels in their cage at night. Tilly didn't think it mattered. He thought it would already be too late for any of his rivals to pinch his idea, even if they spotted the squirrels at this stage. So when night came now he just threw the old tarpaulin over the cage and left them out in the open.

Night came, and still work on setting up the attractions continued under floodlights. The screen surrounding Tilly's designated area was almost complete. There was just one gap at the side which was left open, and at night blocked off by freestanding steel fencing units. This was the section where the punters would enter on the day of the fair, and where the entrance fee would be taken. It wasn't until late that night that all work stopped, the lights were put out, and the men and women retired to bed. It would be an early start in the morning.

With only two days to go now before Knutsford Fair, it would be a day of hard practice for the squirrels too.

And it was then, deep into the night as the Heath fell silent for the first time that day, that the squirrels were found by Barkan the buzzard.

22. SEARCH

Barry had actually spotted them earlier that afternoon.

The day before, he had been up and aloft early, taking advantage of the clear early morning light and the post-dawn thermal updrafts. He gained height with long slow flaps of his great wings.

He was joined by Beryl his mate and together they set about the first task of the day: feeding their three chicks. Cruising effortlessly they eventually soared to about a thousand feet high. From that vantage they could see around a hundred or so of the less well-hidden rabbit warrens dotted about over twenty square miles in the farmers' fields below.

Each of the buzzards targeted a different warren and very soon each was carrying a dead rabbit in their talons back to the nest in their beech copse home.

Barry left Beryl feeding the chicks and returned to the air.

Since talking with his friend the fox Barry had been thinking about the task he'd agreed to undertake. He was as well aware as Luca was that if the squirrels were being kept indoors then he had no chance of finding them. But he had a hunch, call it no more than that; he felt there wouldn't be much point in keeping wild animals indoors, they'd make a mess for one thing. If they were still alive of course. But if they hadn't already been skinned for coats or liquefied into some strange exotic soup, then Barry reckoned they'd be kept outdoors somewhere. And if they were outdoors he'd find them.

Yet he didn't.

Another thing Barry had to think about was whether it would be more likely the squirrels would be kept in an urban environment or out in the country? Again, Barry's instinct was involved in the search choice he made that day. He felt this whole thing had the feel of farmers about it. Who else would bother with squirrels? To Barry it didn't seem that kidnapping squirrels was something that town-living humans would get up to.

For that reason for the whole of the first day Barry concentrated his efforts on the farms spread out below him.

He found nothing.

The whole of that first day there was no sign of any captive squirrels. He'd spent a little longer than at other places scanning the area around where the squirrels had been reportedly snatched. He checked all the farms and orchards and paddocks in that area very closely.

Barry looking the look

He also took a long hard view of the yard area in the industrial zone where Luca told him the squirrels had been kept for a while. The yard was clear.

In another place he dropped down to 150 feet to take a very close look at a squirrel family he spotted playing in some chestnut trees. But they seemed free and carefree and definitely not under the control of humans.

He even saw Luca hiding and resting outside one of his favourite dens, under a bushy hedge next to a reedbed by a small lake which was part of the golf course at Vale Royal.

But he didn't find the squirrels he was looking for.

He cruised an astonishing distance, constantly scanning the ground. Having regained his preferred initial scanning height of a thousand feet, Barry soared over to the suburbs of Manchester to the east. He rose higher in a curving helix to around fifteen hundred feet. He then spent the whole day slowly cruising in five-mile diameter circles on the thermals and moving westwards across the Cheshire Plain, and arrived at the eastern suburbs of Chester, 30 miles west, by late afternoon.

Barry reckoned he hadn't missed a single farm that day in all that distance.

But he found no squirrels.

Concerned, frustrated, piqued and not a little annoyed by the failure of his day's work, Barry returned to his beech copse. He ate some rabbit and chatted about the problem with Beryl.

"Give it up, love," Beryl said. "You've done your bit. Your fox mate can't ask for more than that."

"I said I'd give it two days. And I'll do that. I thought it would be easier than this though. I get a feeling I'm not looking right."

He told Beryl how he'd been concentrating on farms all the way across the Cheshire Plain.

Beryl knew that if Barry hadn't found the squirrels on a farm, then they just weren't there.

"All I can do is cover the ground tomorrow I didn't look at today."

"The towns you mean?"

"Yes. Towns. The villages as well."

"Then at least you'll have done what you said you'd do. They can't expect you to do more than that."

But she saw that Barry had that look. And that look said he

wouldn't give up until he'd found the squirrels. Then Beryl knew that she might have to step in before this got out of hand. She couldn't have him concentrating on this squirrel job at the expense of helping her feed the little ones.

"Just one more day, then?" She said with finality.

"Absolutely. One more day. Then I'll back off, squirrels or no squirrels," Barry agreed.

Next day soon after dawn he was back in the sky, riding the early morning thermals a thousand feet up.

This time he thought he'd work west to east. He started at Chester's eastern suburbs and began to soar over all the small and large villages, and towns, lying east of Chester, spread out on the Cheshire Plain.

He was particularly interested in front lawns and back gardens. He'd suddenly remembered something interesting that Luca had said. He said that the squirrels might have been taken to provide amusement for human children. In which case, Barry thought, they might be being kept in hutches, runs, coops or cages on lawns or gardens, in a similar way to how rabbits were kept by humans.

This time cruising again in great circles, sometimes three miles across, sometimes five miles across, he worked his way east. And eventually by mid-afternoon he came to Knutsford.

There was a lot of activity going on down on the heath there. Barry dropped down to 200 feet to take a closer look.

There were lorries and humans spread out all over the heath. The humans appeared to be engaged in frantic building activities. The alien sounds of banging, drilling and sawing rose up into the sky and assaulted Barry's ears and the vile smell of diesel from innumerable generators assaulted his nostrils.

Barry was about to glide away in distaste and check out the lawns and gardens of the town when suddenly he thought he saw something out of the side of his eye. One of the keenest sets of eyes in the natural world zoomed in to focus on what it was.

Some sort of arena being built in one area of the Heath. A cage on the ground in one corner of it. Grey movement in the cage.

Barry dropped down in a tight helix to only 150 feet above the Heath. Then he saw it.

Squirrels! In the cage there were two squirrels.

The buzzard took a long hard look, committing all the details of the scene below to memory. He saw two german shepherd guard dogs and a jack russell, together with a bunch of humans. Then Barry flapped his wings, increased height and moved back over the country outside the town. He found a small wood and descended to rest in the high branches of an oak tree.

Barry needed to think and assess the situation.

He may have found the squirrels. But were they the right ones? Barry decided there were certain things he had still to do.

Again he returned to his nest to talk with his mate.

"It could be a long night," he said.

"Did you find them?" Beryl responded.

"Could be." He told her what he'd found.

He told her what he planned to do that night. She wasn't that happy about it. But knew she couldn't really object to Barry's plan. She too was aware of the strong demands a deal made on you. And in return who knew in the future what the fox might be able to do for them?

The one good thing about the german shepherds was that though they had been brought by Tools Tilly to the temporary set-up he had established on the Heath, at night the dogs were locked inside one of Tilly's forty-foot containers, now empty of the various components of Tilly's attractions. Which meant that at the dead of night, if you were completely silent, and were approaching from an unexpected direction – in Barry's case from above – then you might be able to get in and out of the compound without anyone being the wiser. The jack russell was in the caravan by the side of the compound with Tilly himself, where they were both as often as not watching telly.

In the dead of night Barry descended on silent wings to the ground just next to the cage.

"Hello O Squirrels," he whispered. "My name is Barkan. I'm a buzzard." But then realising that wouldn't be enough, added. "And I'm a friend."

Under the tarpaulin a trembling voice from inside the cage said. "Hello O Buzzard. Are you sure you're a friend?"

"Yes. Luca the fox sent me."

"Er, sorry we don't know any foxes," Jimmy said.

Barry was disappointed. After all that intense work for two long days, these were clearly the wrong squirrels. But then realised, from what Luca had told him, the whole thing was a little more complicated.

"Well," Barry whispered. "There may be a cat involved."

"A cat?" The squirrel was clearly terrified by the concept.

"Yes. And a dog."

"A dog!" The squirrel's voice was considerably more hopeful. "What kind of dog?"

"I'm afraid I don't know," Barry replied. And then added, "Sorry I think I've got the wrong squirrels." He prepared to launch himself back into the night sky.

"Wait. Wait," Jimmy whispered urgently. "Are you going to tell the fox you found us?"

"Yes I will. Later tonight I hope. It will be up to him to decide what to do next. Nothing I guess if you're not the ones he's looking for."

"And the fox will report back to the dog and the cat?" Jimmy tried to keep his voice flat. He didn't want to sound too hopeful.

"Yes. I guess so," Barry said with finality. "But I don't really know."

"Then please ask the fox to send a message to the dog," Jimmy whispered with complete and desperate urgency. "Just tell him one word. Collar."

"That's all? Just 'collar'?"

"Yes just that please."

"I will do that," Barry said and immediately launched himself into flight. He'd felt too exposed on the ground in that alien place and could wait no longer. He would do as he was asked. To see any caged animal was hateful to him. And he would pass on the message, even if these were not the right squirrels. It was the least he could do.

And now that same night he would cruise west in the sky and locate Luca.

23. REPORT

Barry found Luca still hiding by his den under bushes near the reedbed by the lake on the golf course. There were feathers all round his hiding place and the remains of a duck next to him.

"Hello feller," Luca said as Barry glided in, decelerated and fluttered down next to him. "Hungry? Have a bite. Tuck in."

"I found some squirrels," Barry said as he ripped apart a piece of duck with his hooked beak.

Barry told the fox how he'd been spending the last two days.

"Knutsford Heath, eh?" Luca said.

"Yes. There's a lot going on there, though."

"It's the time of year. The humans have some kind of outdoor celebration and party thing there every year around this time. I've seen it before." Luca had on several occasions enjoyed picking through the leftovers from Knutsford Fair.

"I don't really know if these are the squirrels your friends are looking for." He saw Luca cocking his head to one side at the suggestion he might have such friends. Barry carried on. He explained about the makeshift arena and the cage covered by a tarpaulin. "But there's two of them there in a cage in a compound on the Heath. But who knows if they're the right ones?"

"You didn't see any others? Just those?"

"No. Nothing. Nowhere. One of them did give me a message for you to pass back. He just said 'collar'." Barry said. "I don't know what it means. He just said tell the dog that."

"Not sure I want to be meeting this particular dog at all. But I'll pass that on to the cat. She can do with it as she wishes. Doesn't make any sense to me either. But thanks. You've done a great job. As always."

The buzzard and the fox passed the rest of the night together eating duck by the lake. As dawn came up, Barry said goodbye his friend and prepared to rise up in great soaring flaps into the red-streaked sky.

Just before the buzzard left Luca asked Barry to tell him exactly in more detail whereabouts on the Heath the squirrels were. So Barry told him. Luca also asked what Barry could tell him about the cage the squirrels were kept in. In particular, had he noticed how the cage door was secured?

"It's a just a wire cage, about five feet in length and breadth by maybe three foot high. The door is a simple hook and eye affair. It's held closed by no more than a wooden peg pushed through the eye," Barry explained.

"That's good, at least," Luca said. "And now I better talk to the cat."

He watched his friend reach his cruising height and head east. Luca knew from previous expeditions to Knutsford Heath that the human celebration there, the fair, once it started was only a one-day thing. He assumed the squirrels would be moved to parts unknown as soon as the fair was over. Once they were moved off the Heath, they'd be lost again. Even if these were the right squirrels, time was running short.

24. PLAN

It wasn't until the night came that Luca felt safe enough to move from the lakeside. He made his way towards where the cat lived.

He found her on top of the familiar brick wall, licking her paws. He noticed Max the dog was out in the garden again going about his nightly rounds.

"Who's been a busy vulpes vulpes, then?" He said as he climbed effortlessly up the brick garden wall and moved along the top towards Della. "I've got some news."

He sat on his haunches next to Della and told her everything that had happened since they last met under the ferns in the railway cutting.

"You think it's them?" Della asked.

"I've no idea, love. But they're the only ones for miles and miles around that are in captivity. As far as we know. And I do mean miles." The awe in Luca's voice came through noticeably. The distance the buzzard could cover with relatively little effort was remarkable and astonishing to the fox.

"So it could be?"

"Could be. Might be. Might not be. There's also a message for you to tell yonder dog. Apparently one of the squirrels said: 'Just tell the dog, 'collar'. That's all."

Della looked blank.

"Yes. Just the word collar."

"Maybe we should pass that on to Max," Luca said, gesturing with his snout in Max's direction.

The fox and the cat moved along the top of the wall till they came to a point above where Max was sniffing and investigating around in the bushes.

"Hello Max," Della said. "We've got some more news."

Max looked up at the top of the wall.

"Luca's found the squirrels again." Della said.

"With a bit of help," Luca insisted. "Well a lot of help. And not me at all really," he confessed. "I just set things moving."

"I've no idea if these are the squirrels you're concerned about.

They're a long way away from where they were before. But one of them apparently sent a message for 'a dog'," Della said. "Which could be you. The squirrel said to say 'Just say the word 'collar' to the dog'."

"Ah," said Max. "Yes. I'm the dog. And it's them all right." Then he added "So they are still in some kind of captivity? Can you tell me again where exactly they are?"

The fox explained the situation the squirrels were in, where they were, how they'd been found, and how they could be moved on anywhere very soon and lost again.

"So they're in some kind of exhibition?" Max asked. "Some sort of show?"

"Yes a one-day fair in Knutsford," Luca replied. "You know Knutsford?" he added.

There was only a blank look and a partial shake of the head from the dog. "A bit," he said. "But only from a car window."

Luca looked at Della with his eyes asking the same question.

"Heard of it," she said. "I've a rough idea where it is. I've been part of the way there. But never been all the way."

"What's all this about anyway?" Luca said. "Why d'you want to know where they are?"

"What do you mean?" Max replied. "Of course I want to know where the squirrels are."

"Why? What for?" Luca said. "You don't seem to get it. Once an animal falls under the power of humans, that's it. Forget them. There's no way out. Nothing you can do. It's destiny. Knowing where they are and what's happened to them just makes it worse."

"Luca's right," Della said. "They're gone. You have to let it go. Let them go. It's their fate. There's nothing we can do about it. And Knutsford's a long way to go just to say goodbye."

"It's better in many ways that you don't know what's happened to them and where they are," Luca said. "Remember them as they were."

"Compared to humans, we have no power," Della said. "We might imagine we do. Pretend sometimes even. But we don't. Humans have got them. That's their fate. It's over Max."

"Some humans are great; and most are okay," Max said. "But I agree: some aren't so good. But I'd still like to know all about them. I'd like to know the way to Knutsford too," Max said stubbornly. A new element for Max had been the feeling that had been growing ever since the squirrels had disappeared, which was that humans were very much involved, that somehow humans were letting him down. In some strange way Max felt betrayed.

Luca turned back to the dog. "Why do you want to know anyway?"

"It's not over. Fate is fake," Max said. Then he added: "You don't always have to do what you're supposed to."

That was something different, something new, Luca thought. Not understanding at all what he meant, the fox titled his head slightly on one side and looked at Max.

Della did understand what the words meant. After all, she had set this course of events into motion. But she was now beginning to understand the dangers involved when you didn't always do what you were supposed to. Things could run away out of your control. Anything could happen. And yet she didn't feel trapped and frightened by how things were turning out. She felt exhilarated.

"What does that mean?" Luca asked. "As Della said, Knutsford's a mighty long way to go just to say goodbye."

"It's not about saying goodbye," Max said, looking away into the distance. "I'm going to rescue them," he added quietly.

25. DEAL

Rescue! Luca was astonished. Was that what this was all about? Maybe he should have seen it coming. This dog clearly thought he could do anything. He appeared to believe nothing was beyond him. But if he had no real idea where Knutsford was – and why should he in his cloistered doggy life? – let alone how to get there, then this rescue mission wasn't going to get very far.

And this strange phrase the dog had used – you don't always have to do what you're supposed to – what on earth was that? That was something different, something new all right. Everything'd be in a right mess if animals were no longer predictable. Make deals and arrangements; gain an edge here; give a bit there; get on with the world as far as you could; do to others what you'd have them do to you; and if you couldn't, then make sure you did others before they did you, those were Luca's standards of behaviour. They worked well, and always had. But as soon as everyone didn't do what they were supposed to, then chaos would result. And chaos was no place for a fox. With chaos things could get unpredictable.

The dog was dreaming, obviously. But Luca was not one to puncture another animal's dreams. Or even comment on the way another animal saw the world. Dream and let dream, was Luca's view. If other animals couldn't see reality when it bit them, that wasn't Luca's problem. So let the dog dream.

"Well, I could give you directions I suppose," Luca said hesitantly. That seemed a little far-fetched. Go about a night's march east along this railway line. When you get to a small town, that's Knutsford. Across the town on one side there's a large open grass area called the Heath. On the Heath in some kind of compound is a large cage. In the cage are two squirrels. No, he thought, it's not going to work.

"No," Max said. "That's not going to work."

There was a long silence as the dog and the fox stared at each other. Then out of the silence the cat spoke again.

"I can find it," Della said.

Max looked at her with great – and new - respect.

"I have a better idea," Max said. "Luca I'd like to make a deal

108

with you."

Uh-oh, Luca thought. I shouldn't have hung around here. "What kind of deal?" he said cautiously

"Will you show me the way?" Max asked.

Luca didn't say anything. In the past few days he'd been drawn in to a series of deals that may or may not prove fruitful in the future. But a deal with a dog seemed too much, too far against his nature. But then his deal-making instinct kicked in, and before he could stop himself he asked: "And what if I do?"

"I offer you safety and security in this garden," Max said.

Despite his initial reluctance, Luca's interest perked up.

Max continued: "Come what may, you will always be safe in this garden. This place will become a refuge for you; a sanctuary at all times in all seasons. Once here, if anyone, any dog or any animal of any kind, wants to get at you, they'll have to go through me. They won't like doing that. Believe me, they'll think again."

Luca remembered the short work this bruiser had made of the notoriously troublesome boxer. And Luca believed him. Apparently he sincerely believed he was capable of seeing off a whole pack of foxhounds. And then again, who said he couldn't?

In many ways it was an unbelievably good offer. And anyway, what harm would it do to show him the way to Knutsford Heath? If they met trouble, Luca could always dump the dog and make himself scarce. There was no one better at making themselves scarce.

And yet. And yet, Luca just couldn't bring himself to make the deal. This wasn't the normal kind of deal whereby two animals shared a mutual benefit at minimal risk – where in a way it would be perverse and idiotic not to make the deal. This deal was the other way round: it would be perverse and idiotic to make it. There were also humans involved in this, and Luca didn't want anything to do with them. Too dangerous. Too unpredictable. No, that wasn't it: they were plenty predictable about all that mattered; which was, they killed animals at all and every opportunity. Luca's ultimate motto was: keep clear of humans. Avoid.

In the end Luca's sense of danger and deeply engrained sense of self-preservation made him say no.

"I'm sorry," he said. "It's a great offer. One maybe I'd be mad to turn down. But I have to say no; I can't show you the way to Knutsford. I really am sorry." And he was. He was already feeling guilty about letting them down almost before the words were out of his mouth.

"I completely understand," Max said, which as far as Luca was concerned made it worse.

"Anyway," Max continued, turning to Della. "It's not as bad as it looks. I've been to Knutsford many times. Okay, not on foot but in my humans' car, but I've definitely been there, and could find my way around once I got there. I know where the Heath is, for one thing. I've also been to Knutsford station, by car too, so I know what that looks like and would recognise it again. I'm sure we can do it."

"You don't want to be going anywhere by road, feller," Luca said. "Have you no idea how dangerous they are? Absolute death-traps."

"Well, I know part of the way to Knutsford along the railway line. Part of the way," Della said.

"So, if we combine your knowledge with mine, we should be all right," Max said with finality. "Will you come with me?" He asked Della. "I'm sorry, I don't have the knowledge to get there on my own, especially along the railway. I'd be glad if you'll come. Very glad."

"I will come," Della said.

As soon as she said that, she felt frightened. But she bolstered herself with the thought that if things got rough she would run and hide, and get out it while she could. She could run and hide better than anyone she knew. There was also something else. A little something stirring in her heart. She was inspired by the stubborn intention of the dog to do something about the squirrels. It was probably true, as Luca insisted, that there was absolutely nothing they could do to change the fate of the squirrels. To fall in the power of humans was the squirrels' destiny. But that didn't stop Max from wanting to try to change that. And some deep part of the cat wanted to be part of that attempt too.

She didn't say the reason why she had knowledge of only part of the way to Knutsford was because, when she explored that way in her younger days, her passage had been blocked by a very big, very aggressive, and very nasty tomcat. She hoped the tom was no longer there. *What am I doing?* She thought to herself. *It's crazy.*

"That's settled then," Max said. "Let's do it tomorrow night. The sooner the better. Meet here same time tomorrow?"

Della agreed. *Maybe the sooner is the better,* she thought. *While I've still got the necessary public courage.*

Max turned to Luca. "Thanks for all your help, Luca. I don't know what I'd have done without your help. You really have clarified the situation. We don't have a deal, but I for one will never chase or attack you. You have my word."

"No problem, feller," Luca replied. Then he turned and sped away, saying over his shoulder as he went: "Best of luck." And was gone.

26. JOURNEY

Max spent the day preparing himself for the great expedition he had committed himself to during the coming night.

He was glad the cat was coming. She seemed very resourceful, and without her input he would never have known what happened to his friends Jimmy and Jenny. And who knew, a dog and a cat travelling together might have certain advantages that each travelling on their own might not have?

Once he had committed himself to this rescue project, Max felt happy and content. At least making the rescue attempt was absolutely necessary. It was the least he could do, for without Jimmy's unheard of intervention Max knew he would have died. He owed the squirrel his life. Max felt too that the action of the squirrel was not fate or had been fated to happen in any way. In fact the squirrel's little razor-sharp teeth had probably changed Max's fate that day. Max was convinced that fate had no part in anything. You did what you did, and there were certain consequences, good or bad. But there was no fate. You always had a choice.

He was concerned however that his humans would worry about him when they found him missing. This wasn't going to be like before when he could sneak away for a couple of hours and know his humans would never know he'd been gone. This time he would be gone for more than a day. Perhaps two days. He knew that other bull terriers he had heard of had been kidnapped and sold to gangs staging dog fights. And he knew his humans would fear that had happened to him.

Oh well, there wasn't much he could do about that. And if all went well he would be back in a day, maybe, or a day and a half, two days at the most. He'd make it up to them when he got back.

Last thing at night before they retired to bed, Max's humans always let him out of the house to make his inspection rounds of the big garden. It was raining hard, but Max didn't mind that. Rain always seemed to keep new smells on the ground for longer, and freshen up old ones. Rain seemed to make the world more alive.

Max found Della waiting for him on top of the brick wall.

To Max's everlasting astonishment a slim sleek red shape was also sitting on top of the wall. Had he come to see them off?

"I couldn't let you go on your own," Luca said. "Is the deal still on?"

"Of course," Max said. "You're coming?"

"If we go, we go under certain conditions," Luca said. "I'll be in charge. And on the way you do exactly as I say. Is that clear? It'll be very dangerous; and we'll all be far from home." And Luca didn't say what he knew he would do if necessary, if it came to it. He would leave the others in the lurch and make himself scarce if he had to.

Both Max and Della agreed.

So the dog and the cat and the fox set off in the rain.

They headed to the end of Max's garden, ducked through the shrubs by the willow trees, under the iron fence, and down the bank of the railway cutting to the line. Luca told them they would make best progress on the strip of dead ground alongside the ballast, between the line and the bank. He set off in a punishing pace through the relentless rain. The other two followed side by side right behind him.

"Don't worry if you can't keep up," Luca called over his shoulder. "I'll stop every now and then for a breather, and for you to catch up," he said. "And we'll cross the tricky bits together anyway."

Della didn't think she liked the idea of 'tricky bits', but said nothing.

"I'll keep up," Max said.

"And I'll hear you, however far you get ahead," Della said. "Don't worry about me."

Soon the dog was breathing hard, his tongue lolling out of the side of his mouth, but he kept going strongly and maintained his position just behind the fox. Della was silent, as always, but she was struggling a little to keep up the pace. Luca kept going, his head low and his lean body stretched out, eating up the ground.

Within half an hour they came to the Arches. Luca stopped. His breathing was still quiet and under control. Max on the other hand, though he felt fine, was making a lot of noise. And Della, while still silent, was struggling even more to stay level with her two companions and had fallen twenty yards or so behind.

"The rain's good," Luca said. "A real bonus. No one's going to be out on a night like this if they don't have to."

The black serpentine sentinel of the Arches stretched away ahead of them.

"Do you hear it?" Della asked. "The noise? I think there's a train coming."

"You're right love. Quick, quick, follow me," Luca headed away from the line towards a small brick railway workshed standing on its own a few feet away. The three animals hid behind the back wall of the shed as the train rattled past.

When all was silent again, they returned to the line.

"This is the first of the tricky bits," Luca said. "The Arches. We need to cross this section as fast as possible. A real sprint. We can rest again on the other side. It should take only a couple of minutes if we push it."

"Let's go," Della said and sprang forward. Her companions followed. Luca quickly overtook Della and sprinted on. Max brought up the rear. Running as fast as he could, he still trailed Della all the way across the viaduct.

Panting, all three reached the cover of a bramble covered bank on the far side of the Arches.

"Not sure I could do that again for a while," Della said, completely out of breath.

"Hopefully we won't have to," Luca said. "Let's take a breather."

After five minutes rest they pressed on again. The rain arrowed down like reinforcing bars. Now Luca resumed the loping punishing pace he'd set before. Mile after mile he pushed on. Now even Max fell some way behind him, panting very hard; while Della began to fall some way behind him. Eventually Della was left about fifty yards behind. She wasn't worried too much, her sharp ears could hear Max's puffing a lot further away than fifty yards.

The railway line began a long slow curve to the right, and for a moment her companions were out of sight.

"Hold on, darling," a voice hissed out of the gloom. "Not so fast. Where do you think you're going?" A black shadow slid out of the dark and stood right in front of Della and blocked her progress.

It was a huge black and white tomcat. She halted and then made to veer round the tom, who moved again to intercept her and block her intended route.

"Now that's not very polite, is it darling? Trying to push past me without so much as a by-your-leave. It's a nasty night to be out, and in all of a hurry too."

Della had no choice but to stop again, panting hard, still completely silent, but very much out of breath.

Della realised she had been here before. This was the very same tomcat that had prevented her exploring further along the line a year or so before.

"Well, I never," the tomcat said. "I remember you. You're a great white lovely, aren't you. But you weren't very sociable last time we met either, as I recall."

"Let me pass," Della panted. "I have to keep up."

"Ooh I don't think I will. I don't think so at all. Your pals are long gone by now, darling. Well ahead, I'd say, and well out of it. I don't think they'll be coming back for you. A dog and a fox; now that's a strange business. Very strange. But be that as it may. I think you're on your own now, darling. So now, how about being a bit more friendly?"

"Let me pass!" Della insisted, arching her back, puffing out her wet fur as much as she could to make herself look bigger, and hissing at the tom. "One of my friends will make short work of you when he comes back."

"The fox? You're having a laugh. I eat foxes before breakfast. And the dog? I don't think so darling. I've seen plenty of dogs in my time. All piss and windy bark. Face up to them and they back off. They don't frighten me. Now then, where were we?"

"LET ME PASS! I'M WARNING YOU! LET ME PASS NOW!" Della raised her voice desperately until she was almost shouting.

The tomcat seemed momentarily surprised and nonplussed by the volume, but then said "Warning me is it? Shouting's not going to get you anywhere, darling. That's not going to do you any good. No one's going to hear you. Help's not going to come, you better believe it. Now how's about being a bit nicer and you and me—"

"What's the problem?" a voice said from behind the tom, interrupting his flow. Surprised, he whirled round to face a bull terrier standing right behind him, less than two feet away. The tom moved back another couple of feet: two feet was far too close to a dog.

"None of your business sunshine," the tomcat said. "Just passing the time of day."

"It looks to me like you're blocking my friend's way," Max said.

"Oh yeah? Well what're you going to do about that, pal?" The big black and white cat arched his back and showed all his teeth, snarling and hissing. To Della he looked huge and terrible.

"I don't know what you think you know, but whatever it is, it's not enough," Max said quietly. "I don't know what experiences you've had with dogs, but whatever it is, it's not enough. And I don't know what you think you've got in terms of weaponry and fighting ability; but whatever it is, it's not enough."

The two animals stared at each other, one silent, the other hissing loudly.

The tomcat's confidence wavered slightly in the face of this quiet and calm dog, so different from the loud and excitable dogs the cat had dealt with relatively easily in the past. But he was still sure the aggression and front that had served him so well against other dogs on previous occasions would work now too.

"You dogs make me laugh," he said with wild bravado. "Always needing a human to back you up, or finish the job for you, or get you out of a mess. Well I've got news for you sunshine: no humans here."

"You talk too much," Max said. "If you hadn't been so full of your own voice you'd have heard me coming and would have been better prepared. That'll be the death of you one day."

The dog and cat stared at each other, one silent, the other hissing loudly.

"Get out of the way now and let my friend pass," Max said after a while. His eyes were narrowed to small horizontal slits and his ears were laid tight against his skull. He tensed his front legs and lowered his head.

Suddenly without saying another word, Max charged at the tomcat. He lowered his head further and ducked under the flashing barbed paw the cat whirled at his eyes and rammed the cat right on the side of the chest at full tilt with the top of his head.

The big cat went sprawling sideways in the gravel and rolled over twice before coming to rest, winded, in a puddle. He sprang to his feet, breathing hard, water dripping from his fur, his dignity in shreds and his self-regard outraged. Della took the opportunity of the cleared route to move past both Max and the tom. She stood at a safe distance and turned back to watch. The tomcat now glared and spat and hissed at Max, but stayed where he was, not coming any closer.

"You might think you're tough, and you may well have seen off a few confused dogs in your time. But I'm different," Max said. "You're just a bully, a natural bully. I'm designed for fighting. When I fight there's only two possible outcomes: I either kill or am killed. Therefore I recommend you leave, clear off, get out of the way now while you can. Or I'll kill you. Yet if you think you can take me, then by all means have a go. But I warn you: you're not in my league. Believe it." Max didn't raise his voice. He spoke calmly and quietly, without bragging but with absolute certainty.

The tom believed him. He didn't like it one bit, but he believed him.

"This isn't over," the tom hissed. "You think you've won this battle. But this is war." He operated as a gang on occasion, with two henchcats. He'd go and find them and come back mob-handed and see how the dog coped with that. With that intent he sprang away into the bushes overhanging the line and disappeared into the dark and rain.

"I'll be back," he snarled as his black shape merged into the night.

"That was clever," Max said, calmly approaching Della. He wasn't even short of breath. "Raising your voice and shouting. It masked my approach, didn't it? He never heard me coming. Nice one."

"It was all I could think of. I saw you coming back over the tom's shoulder and was frightened if he saw you he wouldn't run away and there'd be a fight and a lot of noise."

Max was beginning to realise this was a very clever cat indeed.

"You're right, noise is what we don't want."

"What did he mean about 'this being war'?" Della asked.

"Probably he assumes we'll be making our way along here again, and he'll be ready for us next time, I imagine." Max said. "Try to ambush us, I should think. Something like that anyway."

"But we will, won't we?" Della said. "Be coming back this way."

"Can't be helped," Max said, implying that whatever trouble the big tomcat thought he could cause, Max would deal with it.

Max explained that he'd stopped to take a drink from a puddle, and had looked back and though he hadn't seen the big tom, he had noticed that Della had stopped for some reason, and had come back to see if she was all right.

Luca, always completely aware of his environment and what was happening in it, had realised his companions had fallen behind and was now waiting for them some way ahead. They rejoined him.

"Trouble?" Luca said. "Tricky bit?"

"Sorted," Max said.

The line now went through a long passage where it ran on embankments across the plain, above the fields and pastures laid out like counterpanes on either side. Instead of dropping down to the base of the embankment as he normally would, Luca stayed up top alongside the line.

"I don't think anyone'll see us tonight," he said. "And in any case, what does it matter if they do? And if a train comes we can nip down the bank."

They saw no more trains. They didn't know it but it was hours past the time of the last train now.

They raced on alongside the line, the driving rain smiting them from behind as they ran.

They ran grouped together for a stretch. And as when he was here before, at one point Luca switched them to the other side of the line to avoid a badger family. He didn't say anything, just suddenly angled his run and crossed the deserted track and carried on running along the other side. The others followed.

"Why did we just do that?" Max asked Luca as they trotted along side by side. Luca explained about the badger sett.

"Badgers can be really really troublesome and dangerous. Best avoided."

"I agree," Max said. "I'd never want to fight anything that was just defending its own home."

They passed through a couple of stations, quiet and deserted. No one lived there anymore.

Once past Plumley station, Luca slowed down. He wondered how Barry was doing, not far away, up in his beech tree nest with his family. Snug and warm and dry under the leaf canopy, he thought. More sense than I've got, he added to himself.

"I think we can walk for a while now," he said. "It's late. There's no one about. And we've got plenty of time. We've done well."

But even walking they went at different speeds and as the miles went by were strung out along the line.

It must have been about half-past three in the morning when Luca stopped walking and waited for the others to catch up. He waited by a pool of clean rain water held in a depression in the compacted ground. He drank and the others drank too as they came up the track together and joined the fox.

"Light soon," Luca said. "But let's take a short break. We might need all our energies if we're caught out in daylight."

The bull terrier lifted up his long snout and sniffed the air, nodding his head slightly up and down to filter and differentiate the scent molecules hitting his nasal receptors.

"There's a town nearby," he said. "Not far away. Not far now."

They set off again, with a hint of light now appearing in the east. Very soon they came to a huge horse chestnut tree overhanging the railway bank above the iron fence on the left hand side of the railway line. Luca waited for Max to catch up and the pair of them waited for Della to join them. The light was getting stronger and they could see there were playing fields behind the tree, and in the distance a group of one and two-storey flat-roofed buildings with large windows. A school.

"I recognise this place," Luca said. "I have a feeling we can take a short cut here. We can miss out the town altogether. Trouble is, I can't really remember which is the direction to the Heath from here. It's quite a while since I've been this way."

"That's my department," Della said, and though very tired, before either of her companions could react she jumped up onto the trunk of the big conker tree and rapidly made her way up into the high branches and disappeared from sight. The other two waited by the base of the tree.

After a while she scurried back down the trunk and joined them on the ground.

"Yes. There's a large grassy area with a big wheel thing on it at one side. And there are lots of containers and temporary structures, and banners and flags. It's over that way." She indicated towards the school. "It's close," she said.

"Right. That way it is. Better go fast again here." Luca set off at a sprint across the playing fields towards the school buildings. Della overtook Max: when it came to a sprint Max was always going to come third.

They skirted round the school buildings, across the car park in front of them, and under the steel gate at the head of the entrance drive. The turn-in to the school entrance gate was off a suburban road with houses built in the 1930s.

"This way," Luca said. "Quick, but stealthy." It was getting on for broad daylight now, though still no more than the crack of dawn.

They began to move along the pavement by the side of the road. The driver of an electric milk-float couldn't believe his eyes when he saw, or thought he saw, a fox and a dog and a cat trotting swiftly down the road across from his float.

The suburban residential road ended after three hundred yards. Very soon the three adventurers stood at a tee-junction at the head of the residential road. The bigger road now passing left and right in front of them was clearly one of the main routes into the town of Knutsford.

And they looked up. And there, on the other side of the road, right across from where the three animals stood, was Knutsford Heath. It was a large grassy space, but it was almost completely covered by vehicles, stalls, temporary structures, containers, and "attractions". It was all completely still. The only sound on the Heath was the call of birdsong as various species of small male bird championed their right, each in their own distinctive dawn chorus, to own a certain piece of real estate, and be better at singing – and therefore at being a mate – than the other males.

"We made it," Luca said. "Now let's go over there, rest up, and have a conference. We have a lot to talk about." He indicated a thick wooded and bushy area, full of dense undergrowth that lined the whole of the left hand edge of the Heath as they looked at it. The densely wooded band was at least fifty yards thick and as much as a hundred yards thick in places, before it abutted on to the narrow road called Ladies Mile on the very western edge of the Heath.

"Let's find somewhere in that lot to lie up," Luca said, and led the way across the road, onto the Heath, and into the dense undergrowth along Ladies Mile.

They moved into the thick trees, heavy with undergrowth, and found a secluded dark patch of ground in the low bushy undergrowth, hidden from view in all directions.

"We should sleep if we can," Luca said. "But first, what's your plan?" He looked at Max.

"I always thought that if I was going to rescue the squirrels, it would have to be at night. I knew it might take more than one day to carry out. So I guess my plan is to hide up now for the day. Get some good rest. And then late tonight when everything's quiet again, we go and see if we can find the squirrels. Then see what we can see. Either way, with or without the squirrels, we travel back home straight after that, during the night."

"I'm happy with that," Luca said. "What about you love?" He asked Della.

"No one will miss me for a day and two nights. I'm happy with the plan."

"Right then. Let's sleep while we can. But I suspect there'll be a lot of noise soon from over yonder." He nodded towards the Heath.

27. FAIR

The fox wasn't wrong. The fairground that took over Knutsford Heath for the day stirred early. Today was the Saturday of Knutsford Mayday Fair.

Many English villages have had some kind of Mayday celebration, with dancing round a maypole and a May Queen and much eating and drinking, going back centuries. All to celebrate the beginning of summer in a festival that went back to Roman times and before. For anyone knows, this kind of public celebration of the onset of summer may go back to Druid times in the ritual known as Beltane. It would be an unwise person who claimed it wasn't. Anyway, all these celebrations of important events in the rural calendar survived the conversion of England to Christianity. Some of the festivals were actually incorporated into the Christian calendar. As is well known this happened with Christmas.

Beltane too did well for many centuries. But it all began to come to an end in the 17th century with the commitment of large numbers of people in England to the Puritan mindset. The essence of the Puritan mindset is to take what you believe in very seriously. And so in 1644 Oliver Cromwell's Puritan dominated Commonwealth government banned the erection of maypoles. They were condemned as "heathenish", which they undoubtedly were. But until the Puritans arrived in power nobody had cared whether they were heathenish or not.

Centuries later, it was the Victorians who revived many of these medieval relics. Unlike the Puritans, the strong Romantic mindset of the time saw no harm at all, and instead took great delight, in such fascinating ancient folksy folklore mumbo-jumbo as maypoles, May Queens, holly at Christmas, harvest festivals and many another memento from the medieval mind. The Victorian age saw a people looking back to previous ages for much of its art and entertainment. And for the Victorians form became much more important than function.

And so Knutsford fair too is a Victorian revival. Though there may well have been dancing round a maypole in the Middle Ages on Knutsford Heath, the fair started in its modern form in 1864 with a procession through the town to the Heath. There the May Queen was crowned and there was dancing round a maypole. Gradually over the years a number of big wheels, roundabouts, swings, animal rides, machine rides, thrills, exhibitions, freak shows, strikers, shies and shooting galleries were established on the Heath to take advantage of the large crowd gathered that day to watch the crowning of the May Queen. The coming of the Cheshire Lines railway through the town in the 1860s broadened the pull of the Mayday Fair, and the crowds became larger.

Through the twentieth century the fair of the town procession, maypole and May Queen became ever more tightly fused with the funfair of the attractions. Nowadays it is the attractions that bring in and keep the crowds over the course of the day, long after the procession through town and crowning of the May Queen on the Heath is completed.

In the thrill-seeking twenty-first century the crowd that watches the crowning of the May Queen is much smaller than the crowds that compete at the shies and ride on the big wheel and pay to go on and attend all the attractions.

In the twenty-first century who wants to watch some regurgitated rustic ritual or watch morris dancers prance round a maypole when you can win a teddy-bear or go home with a goldfish in a small water-filled plastic bag?

For Tools Tilly and his team of hired hands and helpers it was an early start to the big day.

Tools had dodgems. He had a coconut shy. He had hoops and blocks. He had a strongman striker. He had an air-rifle prize shooting gallery. And now he had what he thought of as his Great Squirrel Race. Tilly's Turns was one of the biggest sets of attractions at the Mayday Fair.

When everyone was up and about, someone lifted off the tarpaulin covering the squirrels' cage. Jimmy and Jenny could watch the action in the compound around them.

They'd had two full days hard practice on the obstacle set-up. Tools had been timing them, and it seemed they were getting faster and faster. That was no bad thing, he thought. It surely meant they could do more runs in the day. And therefore more punters through the gate. And still they were evenly matched. City beat United to the food tray as often as United beat City. If Tools was any judge, and he thought he was, the squirrels looked like they were enjoying it. Familiarity breeds content, he reckoned.

They weren't content, of course. They were just making the best of their captivity and slavery. And trying to keep out of the way of Sid and Dick. And keep Snough as happy as they could, or at least keep on his good side (if he had one).

Generators began to start up, powering those attractions that needed electricity. Lights blinked on and off. Bells rang. Equipment and moving parts were tested. Final adjustments were made. Tools tested the sound system one last time. Tools and his hands were as ready as they could be. Of course, Tools and Ron and Ray, and a couple of the other hands, had been at Knutsford Fair many times. They knew what to do and when to do it.

The Mayday procession processed through Knutsford to the Heath. The May Queen was crowned to a ripple of applause from the sizeable crowd. There was some knee-slapping dancing and prancing round the maypole with the morris dancers attached to the top of the maypole by gaily coloured ribbons and streamers.

Then it was time for the attractions. The fair was over. Let the funfair begin.

It was a long day for all the humans involved in Tilly's Turns. A hot day too, for the May weather was warm and sunny. It was also a money-spinning day.

The shooting galleries always went well. The dodgems were regularly popular. And the strongman striker was always a good puller. Best of all, it was a crowd-puller because there was something addictive not only about taking part but also something very pleasing and attractive about watching someone pit his strength with a big mallet trying to launch the puck up the pole to strike the bell. There was humour in it too. There was something laughable in seeing a hairy-armed farm labourer or car mechanic wield the weighty two-fisted maul in a mighty swing way over his head, bring the mallet down on the striker with a great crash, only to see the puck rise a contemptible two or three feet up the pole. And even more, the laughable contrast of the complete weed, perhaps an accountant or articled lawyer or other spiny-armed office worker barely able to lift the mallet, struggle to lift it then let it drop lightly on the striker-plate, only to witness the puck whizz up the pole and smack the bell with a loud and raucous and somehow ironic clang. It was all very tricky and mysterious, and very addictive, both to attempt and to watch others attempt. Time and time again.

And for Tools Tilly the good thing about a crowd was that once you had it, it was in a sense captive, and you could then direct it towards Tools's latest attraction, the Great Squirrel Race. And the crowds duly rolled in to see what it was all about. They paid to get in. And many of the crowd found a bet or two irresistible on whether City would finally beat United; or whether United would keeping beating City. And they were not disappointed.

Tools Tilly was there, mastering the ceremonies. He stood on an electric hoist platform attached to the back of a lorry, armed with a microphone. He raised the hoist about twenty feet in the air and could look down and comment on all that happened in the Great Squirrel Race below.

The final modification Tools had made to the Great Squirrel Race was to add a small flag to each of the sections of polycarbonate pipe that were the start points of the race course. Now a small red or blue flag fluttered above each tube. This would be the starting point for each squirrel. Ron stood at one end of the run by a start tube, and Ray stood by the side of the other tube. Both squirrels had been emptied from their bags into the back end of the tubes. The squir-rels could be seen clearly through the clear plastic of the start tubes with what Tools thought was their rather fetching blue and red col-lars. And now Ron and Ray stood ready to flip open the front door of the tubes simultaneously at Tools's command. Before that Tools would make the introductions and announce the next race.

"On my left in the blue corner with the blue collar: City!" A chorus of cheers and boos greeted this information.

"And on my right, in the red corner with the red collar: Unit-ed!" Cheers, whistles, catcalls and boos and groans again greeted this announcement.

"First one to the food table is the winner. Will it be City or will it be United? Ladies and gentlemen, boys and girls, take your pick!"

Ron and Ray had become quite adept at handling the squirrels during all the days of practice. And as Tools announced City! and United! they each pointed in exaggerated fashion towards the respective squirrel in the tube next to them. The red and blue collars could be seen quite clearly, and it was obvious which squirrel was which. But apart for the coloured collars the squirrels looked identical. Even Ron, Ray and Tools couldn't tell them apart.

"The last race was very nearly our first dead heat," Tools announced. "But it was won in the end by United," he boomed over the microphone. "Just." The crowd cheered and booed. "It surely must be City's turn now!" More cheers and boos. Whistles. Cries of "Go for it," and "Yes," and "No way," and "Dream on." Then Tilly waited a while for his hands to move through the crowd offering odds and taking bets. Then when he thought it was time: "Release City! Release United!. Go City! Go! Go United! Go!" He shouted. Ron and Ray opened the tube doors and the squirrels ran.

Huge cheers and boos followed their every move along the course. When City waited too long on the seesaw-board, and had to wait for the balance to right itself before jumping on to the next platform, there were groans from a large section of the crowd (accompanied by such gems from Tools as "Bad miss there sunshine. Better get your skates on."). And when United seemed to hesitate at the entrance to one of the long polycarbonate tubes on the course, allowing City to catch up and overtake, there were more groans and hopeful cheers (plus Tools's commentary saying "Back in the saddle, my son. Go for it. Go. Go. Go.").

And so City did often beat United. And United kept beating City. No one in the crowd really noticed that the number of wins for each squirrel was about the same. But Tools did. And he was very pleased. He saw that it was good.

Tools also took care each time, when announcing the preliminaries to the next race, to assure the crowd that he'd had the squirrels right from the time they were "kits" This provoked laughter, so he responded with the information that this was the correct term for a young squirrel. He'd found them young, alone and starving after their parents had been killed, he said. He'd rescued them; fed them; and looked after them when they were abandoned; and given them a new home. He stressed that there was no cruelty involved in the race and the squirrels very much enjoyed taking part in the Great Squirrel Race.

"We never had to train them," he claimed. "As you can see, they just do it naturally." Implausible as this sounded, no one demurred. The squirrels certainly didn't look as though they were unhappy or were trying to avoid running the course or were attempting to escape.

No one in the crowd noticed a little jack russell dog, sitting by himself by a large wire cage in the corner of the arena glaring at the squirrels. At the end of a race, the squirrels were hooked by the collar ("Make sure you do it gently. Gently does it," Tools had told Ron and Ray before the fair), bagged and put back in their cage. Each time the squirrels arrived back in the cage, the watching jack russell just said "Deadmeat" to them in a snarly whisper.

It went on and on all day. Race after race. Race: rest. Race: rest. Cage: bag: tube: race: hook: bag: cage. Race after race. Every half hour on the hour and on the half. With just an hour break for lunch. During the break, with the arena empty, Tools switched the red and blue collars on the squirrels' necks. He didn't think it made a difference, the squirrels were so evenly matched. He did it basically because he could. And he did it because his instinct was always to try to cheat the punters, even if in this case switching the collars gave him no real advantage. It just felt the right thing to do.

After lunch the portable fence was moved from the gate, the punters invited back in the arena, and the Great Squirrel Race restarted.

By early afternoon word had got round the entire fairground that the best attraction among all the attractions that day was the Great Squirrel Race. People leaving the Heath often mentioned to newcomers arriving the delight and fun of the Great Squirrel Race and the incredible acrobatics of the squirrels. Soon there was a queue to get into the arena. Some punters were actually shut out and had to wait at the head of the queue to be first in for the next race. It was full house after standing-room only after full house. Another thing Tools had done was to site the Great Squirrel Race arena along the roadside edge of the Heath, so motorists and walkers along the pavement on their way to the fair could read the posters as they passed, and already be interested and attracted even before they entered the Heath.

It was definitely all that Tools Tilly had imagined it would be. The investment had paid off. Handsome, very handsome, he thought with great satisfaction. He had visions of taking the Great Squirrel Race to all the fairs and county shows in the calendar, all round the country from Frampton in the southwest to Hexham in the north.

At last it was the final race of the day. One last time the exhausted squirrels were made to run the obstacle course. City won, to great delight and cheering from certain sections of the still surprisingly large crowd. When it was over the squirrels were hooked by the collar, bagged, and deposited back in their cage. One final time, Tools's henchmen counted the money from the losers and paid out the winnings to the punters who had won their bets; the former always more than the latter. Then the crowd made its way out of the arena. The portable fence barrier was carried into place to close off the gap. The Great Squirrel Race was over for that Mayday Fair.

Tools and his team retired to his large caravan for a celebratory drink.

"To the Great Squirrel Race," Tools raised a toast. "Long may it last and long may it pay." The lager flowed.

"Early start in the morning lads," Tools said. Some but not all of the hands would report for duty in the morning to begin the long day's work of dismantling all the parts and sections of the various attractions and packing them away in the forty-foot containers. But tonight, after some serious drinking, they would all rest. It was party time.

28. RESCUE

Over in the woody shrubby bushy nettley borderland between the Heath and Ladies Mile, the fox and the cat and the dog slept and rested through the entire day under the close cover of their hiding place.

The noise all day had been tremendous. There were shouts and bangs and whistles and screams and hoots, and clangs and clongs and clanks and clunks, and everywhere the thumping bass notes of all sorts of music, all set within the great shrieking murmuring hubbub that a big crowd of humans makes. But they still managed to sleep through part of it. And when not sleeping, they were still resting their tired bodies and recuperating.

They were waiting for night to come.

And when night did come it was a bright starlit night under a broad full moon. The rain of the night before had not been repeated. They waited until all was quiet on the Heath.

Many of the fairground men had closed away and locked up their attractions, or partially dismantled them, and had then departed. There weren't many that stayed the night on the Heath once the fair was over. But Tools Tilly did. He stayed the night in his caravan at the side of all his attractions, at the back of and behind the Great Squirrel Race arena. He checked on the watchdogs Sid and Dick inside one of the forty-foot containers and made sure they had plenty of water. Then he and Snough retired to the caravan. He drank more lager and watched telly for a while. Then about one o'clock in the morning he too retired to bed.

Half an hour or so later the three animals hiding on the edge of the Heath began to stir.

"I have an idea where they're kept," Luca said. Barry the buzzard had given him information about the squirrels' whereabouts. "We won't have to scour the whole site."

He led the way with extreme stealth and caution to the squirrel arena. The only sound they made between them was Max's breathing, always louder than his companions, but even that couldn't have been heard much further than a few feet away. The three animals arrived at the poster-festooned screens. They moved on until they arrived at the entrance way. Each of them slid easily under the portable barrier blocking the entrance.

By the light of the moon they could see a large open-mesh cage in the far corner of the arena. A tatty tarpaulin partially covered it.

Now Max led the way. As he approached the cage he ducked his nose under the lower edge of the tarpaulin and lifted it up. He looked into the cage.

Two very still and very frightened (and very tired) squirrels stared silently back at him.

"Hello Jimmy. Hello Jenny," Max whispered. "Don't say anything. Absolutely no sound, okay? These are my friends. We've come to take you home."

While he was talking Luca and Della were examining the door to the cage and the way it was secured. A wooden peg was pushed into an eye which prevented a loop from passing over the eye and allowing the door to swing open.

"I get it," Luca whispered to Della. "Now, can you just push with your paw the narrow end of that wooden plug this way a bit?" He indicated where he wanted her to push. "That'll just be enough to give me a start."

Della saw what he meant. She reached out her paw and tapped the peg back in the direction Luca had said. The peg slid slightly backwards. It was just enough to allow Luca to get his teeth onto the larger end. Very slowly and gently he eased the peg out of the eye, pulled it clear, and spat it out on to the ground.

"Now," he said to Della. "Can you flip back that loop with your paw?"

Again she did as Luca suggested. Under pressure from her delicate touch the loop fell back on its hinge. The mesh door now completely unsecured fell open too.

The squirrels would be free in half a second!

And as the door fell open under its own weight it made a loud creaking and squeaking noise as metal rubbed on metal without the benefit of lubrication.

That relatively slight noise in the silence of the night sounded like a troop of baboons spotting a hungry leopard at feeding time.

It was enough to alert Sid and Dick inside their steel container that some kind of untoward mischief might be taking place on their patch. They immediately started barking with an urgent what's-going-on, who-goes-there, let-us-out-to-check-it-out tone.

"Quick, quick," Max said. "Jimmy jump out. Jump out."

Both squirrels jumped out of the cage and landed on the floor just as the light in Tilly's caravan snapped on and Snough began to add his higher-pitched yapping to the racket already being produced by Sid and Dick.

"Out of here. Now. Let's go," Luca said. "Follow me."

Luca ran towards the edge of road that ran alongside the Heath. Momentarily he looked across the main road to the residential street and the distant school beyond, from where they had approached the Heath the night before. But then he changed his mind.

"This way," he said.

Instead of crossing the road he turned left and started running towards the centre of Knutsford. Della ran behind him together with the squirrels who were doing their best to keep up. Max brought up the rear, looking back every now and then over his shoulder.

Amid the commotion raised by the dogs, and though hampered by the effects of having drunk nine large cans of lager earlier in the night, Tools Tilly was quick enough out of his bed in the caravan to spot through the window his now prized possessions the two squirrels making off at speed towards the centre of Knutsford in the company of a dog, a cat and a fox. Too incandescent with anger to really take in that strange combination, he leaped out of the caravan in his tee-shirt and shorts and trainers, only to curse and disappear back inside. He re-emerged carrying the keys to the padlock fastening the chain on the door of the container where Sid and Dick were still making their racket. He was now also carrying a shotgun.

At the same time that Tools first emerged from the caravan, so did Snough the jack russell. He shot between Tools's legs on the caravan step and immediately set off in pursuit of the escaping squirrels.

It took only a moment or two for Tools to unlock the padlock and open the steel door and release Sid and Dick from the forty-foot container. The two german shepherds leapt forward in full pursuit of the escapers, now some way ahead but still in sight. They didn't need to be told who or what to chase. Instinctively they would pursue anything they could see that was running away.

Luca leads the escape

Tilly and the shotgun followed at a wheezing jog, his head throbbing and his belly quivering with the unaccustomed effort.

Luca's idea was that they'd be safer somehow in the streets of Knutsford than they would be crossing the open country of the school playing fields. He wasn't sure why, but he felt the streets gave added protection which the open fields would not. With the shorter sightlines in the town he half-hoped they could confuse, and even lose, their pursuers quite quickly if they were lucky. He was certainly leading his friends back to the railway line. But he was now doing it right through the centre of the town, heading for the train station. Della, Jimmy and Jenny, and Max followed his lead.

The fox lead them across Canute Place, then slightly right into Princess Street, what everyone around calls "the top street". A car drove along the street, a pair of late revellers aboard, but the driver and passenger didn't notice the outlandish collection of animals hurtling along the street almost beside them.

Max looked back over his shoulder and saw the two chasing german shepherds were now crossing Canute Place. There was no sign of the human.

Luca led them on. Leaving Princess Street he turned left abruptly down the cobbled street of Church Hill. At the tee-junction at the bottom of the cobbles, where Church Hill met King Street, what everyone around knows as "the bottom street", Luca turned right. Now the station was in sight!

Where the railway line ran in a bridge above King Street there was a narrow cream coloured gate with stout cream-coloured palings by the side of the street. This allowed pedestrian access up a path and a flight of steps to the line itself and the station platforms above.

Nowadays with unmanned and untenanted stations, the pedestrian gate is not kept locked. That night under the full moon it stood open. Luca led Della and the squirrels through the gate and up the steps as fast as they could go.

Max stopped at the gate. He looked back. The two german shepherds were approaching, not that far away. Their human was in sight too. He had just turned the corner into the bottom street at the bottom of the cobbled Church Hill, panting and wheezing heavily, and no more than walking now, with occasional breaks into a human kind of trot. He stopped frequently to cough ferociously and spit. He was carrying some kind of stick-thing that Max was pretty sure he didn't like the look of. Max knew that something had to be done, and done quickly, to throw off the pursuit.

"Keep going. Keep going," he called up the steps to the others as they waited at the top. "I'll catch you up."

Della looked at Luca. Her first thought was that Max had injured himself in some way and needed to stop.

"What shall we do? Is he all right? Shall we go back and help?" She asked the fox.

Luca knew better. Much more experienced in the dynamics of the chase than the cat, he knew what Max intended to do. He knew that Max knew what needed to be done if the others were to escape. Luca immediately accepted the situation without worrying what was going to happen to Max. That was the way it had to be.

He didn't reply to Della. He didn't want an argument just at this stage.

"Quick, quick," he said, jumping down from the platform on to the line. "Follow me. Keep going."

The others followed. But Jimmy suddenly realised what was going on. He stopped on the edge of the platform.

"No. Wait," he said. "We have to go back for Max."

Luca turned back. "This is what he wants," he said. "Whatever happens, he's buying us time."

"But he's on his own," Jimmy wailed. "Alone. There are so many of them."

Luca thought: and if we go back to try to help him, we'd as like as not just get in his way.

"We have to go little feller," he said as gently as he could. "We really do. Come on." He turned and raced away along the track.

Jimmy stood bereft on the platform edge. Looking up at him from the track, Jenny's heart went out to him.

"You'll see him again," she said.

Jimmy hesitated a moment longer. Then with a tiny whimper, leaped down and joined his sister on the track bed.

As fast as they could, the four animals headed west into the night along the moonlit railway track, the two squirrels hopping and jumping along from one sleeper to the next. The steel rails glinted in the moonlight.

29. GATE

Max took a quick look round. The gateway was actually a good place to make a stand. Not bad at all, he thought. It'll do. Narrow enough so that only one dog could attack at a time. Or if they did try to attack simultaneously through the gap, they would only hamper each other. Either side of the gate, the stout cream-coloured paling fence reached uninterrupted to the red brick back-garden wall of a house on one side, and to the strong Staffordshire Blue bricks of the railway bridge on the other. The fence prevented anyone by-passing Max. The only way through was by the gate.

While level at the gate, the path sloped upwards from there. This gave Max a height advantage too. Max felt back slightly with a hind leg until he touched the riser of the first step. That was good. That would act as a final backstop if he was pushed back. It would also give him something to push off and make a better start position when he lunged and attacked. As he knew he would. He stood in the gate. He drew his ears down till they were flat on his head. His eyes narrowed into tight slits. He crouched a little on slightly bent front legs. He was ready.

But the german shepherds weren't the first dogs to arrive at Max's defensive position. That was Snough. He took one look at the imposing bull terrier standing in the gateway and quickly darted aside, squirmed under the bottom of the fence between the gate and the bridge, and was away up the path and steps before Max could react. Snough sped on after the escaping squirrels.

Max had no time to worry about the jack russell, or even shout a hurried warning to the others before the german shepherds were at the gate.

Max could see they were sizing him up; perhaps wondering why he was stood there in the gateway and had not kept running like any normal dog.

"Get out of it," Sid said, approaching Max, but as yet keeping his distance. "You're not going to hold us up. And we're not stopping. The hunt is on."

"Yeah, that's right," Dick said in back-up. "We're hunting."

But despite their words, both Sid and Dick stopped and panted and looked at the brindled, black and white dog blocking their way.

Max assessed the opposition. Sid was bigger and stronger of the two. He looked older and more experienced. Both dogs were big. But Max thought they looked a little short on power, especially at the back end. Their back legs seemed inadequate somehow and out of proportion to their front ones. They certainly looked as though they weren't capable of giving the dogs the kind of sustained driving power that's needed in a fight. These dogs were all front and no back.

They were also a bit long haired too, Max thought. They looked big, sure, but how much of that was actually hair and how much was muscle?

In the background up the street, a couple of hundred yards and more back, Max could see the human was also coming towards them. Max knew he was running out of time. Max knew that any dog fight goes better without human involvement. They complicate matters, and not least, often make dogs behave unpredictably. Max knew they also made dogs carry on fighting even when they were beaten. Max knew he had to sort this one out before the human got involved.

One of the conventional wisdoms in a dog fight, when one dog is faced with two opponents, is to ignore the weaker dog and attack and kill or disable the stronger and more dangerous dog first. This may on its own be enough to discourage the weaker dog from carrying on the fight.

On this occasion, with these two opponents, Max wasn't so sure that conventional wisdom was right. He had a feeling he needed to do something different this time. Though he knew that time was desperately short, Max felt he had to say something. If nothing else, it may make his two opponents less certain of themselves.

"You need to think about this a bit more," he said with a growl, "before we begin. I can see that you're both generalist, multi-talented individuals. Up for the odd scrap, I'm sure. And that's good. As far as it goes. But I on the other hand am a specialist. This is what I do. This is me. I'm made for this. This is what I'm designed for. My body is designed for damage limitation. Once we start I won't stop until you are dead. Do you fight like that? I don't think you do. I don't feel pain like you do. I can ignore it. Once this begins, unless you run away at some point you won't get out of this alive. You need to think about this. Both of you."

Max holds the gate

For the first time Dick looked worried and uncertain. But Sid scorned Max's words.

"Don't listen to him. He's bluffing," he said. "We're bigger than him. We'll soon send him off."

"You still don't get it, do you?" Max said. "There's no sending off here. There's no noisy brief tussle and scuffle and then backing away, honours even. If you do this fight, you'll die. You have to know that. It's only fair."

As he spoke Max felt the joy of imminent combat coursing through his system. He felt fulfilled, serene and totally content, even happy. This was what he did. This was what he was for. Very few organisms reach that point of fulfilment, where there are no more questions, only certainties. Where the universe slows right down to a zero-moment and they are at the centre of it. But Max had it then. And if he died now, doing what he did best, then that was good too. No organism or being can ask for more than that.

Then, realising he was out of time, Max changed tack.

"Oh all right," he said. "Maybe I am bluffing. Can't blame me for trying. I didn't really fancy fighting you two anyway. A bit out of my league. I'm not really in the mood for a fight. I was only going through the motions. I'll be on my way."

Then Max started to do something very strange. He fell silent and he started to jump in circles. He jumped forward in the air, kicking out his back legs as he leapt. And each time he jumped he didn't land in the same place from where he took off, but a good few inches to his left. He repeated this a number of times, each time landing further to the left, so progressing in a circle. And it was the sixth jump that would have completed the circle and land him at the same place from where he started.

The two german shepherds were mystified by this display. They'd never seen anything like it before. Inevitably as they watched, perplexed and mesmerised, their defences relaxed. This was exactly what Max's circle-dance was intended to achieve.

"He's lost it," Dick said. "Completely lost it. Barking."

Sid wasn't so sure. But he had to agree it was the strangest and most unaggressive prelude to a dogfight he'd ever seen. Like Dick, he just didn't get it; and like Dick he too relaxed his readiness for battle. It looked harmless.

And now in front of them, in the gateway, in his frantic circle-dance as Max took off in the air for the sixth time, instead of landing to complete the circle he changed direction in mid-air, powered by the pistons of his back legs, and he leapt forward to his left and took the smaller german shepherd's neck in a tight grip with the front of his teeth. This was a special slashing, rapidly disabling grip, that is designed to rip and tear, not immediately kill. Max jerked his jaws sideways once, then released his grip. Dick yelped and shuffled backwards, out of the firing line, blood pouring massively from the nasty lines of deep, but not fatal, tears in his throat.

Max was immediately back in his start position in the gateway. He tensed his legs, and held his head low. Blood was dripping from his jaws. It wasn't his blood. Using the riser of the step behind him as a strong leverage point, he lunged forward with all the power of his back legs, up and under the second, and bigger, german shepherd's defences.

He repeated the attack he'd just carried out on the smaller opponent. Sid reeled away, blood pouring from his neck. But he didn't give up. He roared defiance and leapt back at Max, eyes glaring. Max leapt forward at the same time. The two dogs drove into each other. Sid gripped the top of Max's head in his jaws. Max shook him off, the german shepherd's teeth leaving score marks right across Max's skull from ear to ear. Momentarily the two dogs backed off and then leapt forward again. This time Max's powerful back legs kept him driving forward. And he discovered he was right about the weak back legs of the german shepherd. Even though he was a bigger dog, Sid could not resist being driven back and uplifted by Max's torpedo-like power as he bored into him from below. Sid desperately sought some part of Max he could get a hold of, and took a strong grip with his jaws on the only part of Max that was available, his right front leg, just around the foot. As Max inexorably pushed him upwards and backwards, Sid bit as hard as could on the end of Max's leg. Max felt one, perhaps two, of the small bones in his foot break. Max ripped his foot out of Sid's jaws, the german shepherd's teeth dragging great lumps of skin and flesh from Max's foot as it came free. Max ignored the great surge of pain and kept the pressure on Sid, driving him up further and higher and exposing his throat. And as Sid was pushed into the air, his front legs off the ground,

Max lunged his head forward, jaws open, and caught him by the throat in his deadly full-jawed deep killing grip. He sank back to the ground, pulling Sid with him, then planted his feet squarely and ragged Sid's throat, side to side, side to side, side to side. Sid whimpered once, and quite soon Sid lay still.

Covered in blood, Max turned on Dick who throughout the second part of the fight had been keeping a safe and watchful distance. As Max readied himself to deal with him again, Dick turned and fled down the street under the railway bridge and was lost from sight.

Max saw the human was still over fifty yards away, but now shouting and breaking into his flat-footed fat-bellied run again. He had never got close enough to become involved in the fight and take control of his dogs. Max turned and hopped up the path. And even on three legs, he almost sauntered his way up the steps to the platform above. "Tirra lirra, by the railway," Max hummed to himself.

Just as he cleared the top step, a huge blasting swarm of ferocious dog-eating tiny spherical steel wasps took over his head.

Just as Max was almost out of sight, Tools Tilly had managed to get off one shot from the shotgun. And even though he'd heard much of the shotgun blast slamming into the brick side-wall of the ticket office above, Tools thought that enough of the pellets had made contact with the dog. Probably more than enough.

The pellets shredded Max's left ear, vaporising part of it and leaving the rest in ribbons. They ploughed into the skin and dug deep into the flesh along the top of his head, some of them bedding into the thick bone below. Already unstable on his three working legs, Max was knocked off his legs forward on to the platform. Dazed, he shook his head, but the ringing in his left ear didn't go away. It drowned out every other sound. He stood again and carried on, not even deigning to look back at the human who had launched the vicious steel wasps. Blood was streaming down the front and left side of his head. It was dripping into his left eye. He kept shaking his head to clear it. But the blood kept coming. His head hurt quite a bit. His right front foot was mangled and in a terrible state. But other bull terriers had known worse, his mum always told him when he hurt himself as a pup; and he repeated that to himself now.

Max hopped and ran as best he could along the platform and joined the track at the far end where the platform sloped down. He smelled the ground. His friends had passed this way, and they had gone in this direction. He set off on his three legs along the line after them. A dotted line of blood showed where he'd been.

Tools Tilly broke the shotgun open and made sure there was a cartridge loaded in the other barrel, snapped it shut and peered up the station steps, but the dog had gone. Wearily, wheezing and coughing, he dragged himself up the path and the steps to the station platforms above. When he emerged on the platform he expected to see a dead or badly injured dog there, but there was no sign of any animal in any direction. He thought he heard yapping away in the distance which could be coming from Snough, but it seemed a long way away.

Tools realised it was time to call it a day. Without the dogs, he wasn't going to footslog it along the railway line, especially in the dark, and without the dogs he knew he had no chance of recapturing the squirrels anyway. And to what purpose? His anger was dissipating as his breathing began to return to normal and the wheezing became fainter.

He stopped on the platform and took stock in his mind. He'd proved the principle and concept of the Great Squirrel Race worked in practice, what did it matter if these two particular squirrels legged it? Though how they'd managed it beggared belief. He was also worried that someone may have heard the shotgun being fired and may have already got on the phone to the police. More and more he thought he ought not to be in the area. He ought to be back in his caravan, all innocence if anybody came knocking. In his mind he was already writing those two particular squirrels off. It was likely that there were plenty more where they came from anyway. Ron and Ray would just have to get him some more. The Great Squirrel Race would have to find a new City and a new United. Easily done thought Tools, and gave up the chase.

He turned round and descended the steps. He checked out Sid and confirmed that he was dead. To tell the truth, he wasn't too upset or worried about the fate of the two german shepherds. They really were just anonymous guard dogs. He'd just get, or steal, some more. Better get dobermans next time he thought. Real guard dogs. He'd seen the other dog Dick running off madly under the bridge. He thought he might even find his way back to the compound when he calmed down. Failing that, it was likely someone would probably take him in or hand him in to a dogs' home. And if he was already dead, or died later, there was nothing about him that could connect him to Tools.

He was right. Much later that same day a kindly carpenter and his wife, living in a cottage on the outskirts of Knutsford on the Macclesfield road, found Dick hiding under a bush in their garden, exhausted and dehydrated, wounded, very stressed, and very glad to see two very friendly humans. They took him in and he became their own. They gave him a new name too. Neither dog nor humans ever regretted it.

It was Snough Tools was more concerned about. He had a soft spot for the jack russell. In many ways the ferocious persistent little devil reminded him of himself. The yapping in the distance seemed to have stopped. Oh well, he thought, he's a sensible dog. When all the excitement's over, he's likely to find his way home. He'd been away for a couple of days before and still found his way home. With this consolation Tools turned and walked rapidly back up the street towards the Heath, trying to conceal the shotgun by holding it tight against his side as best he could.

30. RESCUE

While Max was holding the gate against the german shep-herds, Snough the jack russell had dodged past him, had leaped up the steps up to the station platforms, and had gone charging along the track after the traitorous escaping squirrels and their deviant treacherous friends. They'd pay. Oh yes, they'd pay. Deadmeat all right. He was rapidly closing the gap.

Della heard him yapping and turned round to look. Luca and the squirrels joined her. They were all very much out of breath.

"I'll handle this," she said to Luca. "You keep going. Go on. I'll be all right. I can look after myself. You look after the squirrels."

Luca wasn't sure Della could handle a jack russell, but didn't say so. And when the dog got past her, what then? He doubted he could handle a jack russell either. They were fearsome committed little beasts, in many ways a miniature version of Max. Well, he said to himself, if he gets past Della, maybe Max will have caught up by then and will be able to help. But he also thought Max wouldn't be coming. He thought that this time Max had probably met his match. It wasn't just two aggressive german shepherds, it was a hu-man with a shotgun too. Well, he thought, cross that bridge when we come to it.

"Come on," he said to Jimmy and Jenny. "Put some distance between us and them." Together the three of them disappeared into the darkness.

Privately Della wasn't so sure she could handle a jack russell either, but she couldn't see what else they could do. She stopped and turned back, facing the oncoming Snough. She hissed, opened her mouth wide to show her small dagger-like teeth, puffed out her fur and arched her back. She hoped she looked big and nasty.

The jack russell stopped running, stopped yapping, and walked confidently up to her.

"You look big," he said. "But you don't look nasty."

Della tried to arch her back even higher and she hissed even more loudly.

"That snake act might work with mice and small birds, and maybe an occasional ageing tom; but it doesn't work with me. Get out of my way, snowdrop," Snough said. "Or you'll regret it. Those squirrels are dead meat. I don't have time for this."

He advanced towards her. Della said nothing, but as he came in range she lashed out at his eyes with a barbed paw with unbelievable speed. But Snough was even faster. He darted his head back out of the way of her clawed paw equally swiftly. The tip of just one of the cat's claws raked along the side of his nose, causing a small but painful scratch.

"Close; but not close enough, snowdrop," Snough said in a surprisingly calm and matter-of-fact tone, licking the dripping blood off his nose. "Don't say I didn't warn you." He flexed and lowered his front legs slightly, ready to spring forward at the cat. She too was deadmeat now.

At that moment there was a whoosh and a whirr of wings, and a blurry flash of brown and white from somewhere in the air. Instantly Snough found himself caught tightly by a series of powerful talons on his back. Then he was being carried into the air. He wriggled and struggled, trying to give himself room to bite at the clawed bird's feet holding him solidly in their grip.

"Struggling and wriggling not advised," a polite voice said. Barry the buzzard continued: "You are probably at the limit of my lifting capacity. In fact you might even exceed it. Wriggling about neither improves my grip on you, nor does it help my flying capabilities. Wriggling and struggling seriously affects my trim. Cut it out."

Snough ignored the advice and kept on trying to contort and arch and turn and attack the feet attached to his back.

"Let me put it another way," Barry said. "Keep still or I'll drop you. Now."

As they were now about thirty feet in the air, Snough decided to keep still.

"That's better," Barry said. "Now I propose we make a deal."

Snough was surprised at that. He assessed the situation. "Not sure I'm in a position to make a deal," he said.

"Oh, I think so," Barry said. "I definitely think you are. Though to tell the truth, I think it's more of an ultimatum on my part than a deal."

They were now about forty feet up in the air. Up ahead Snough could see they were approaching the dark waters of Tatton Mere, a silver strip along the middle of it reflecting the moon.

"This is what I propose," Barry said. "If you promise, and give me your word, now and instantly that you will give up chasing my friends down there, I won't drop you on the road or other deadly hard surface from a very deadly height. Instead I'll drop you from a safe height into the mere there."

Snough was thinking: I could make the promise this daft bird wants. But when he drops me in the water and as soon as I swim to the shore of the mere, I'll follow the deadmeat squirrels' scent again. A promise made under duress is not a promise you have to keep. The bird won't be any the wiser. Until it's all too late.

"Bear in mind that I'll be watching you. And if however you go back on your word," Barry continued. "And again take up the chase of my friends, I will snatch you up again and drop you again. Next time though it won't be in the nice soft waters of the mere."

Snough sensed the inevitability of defeat in the situation he was in. Then he also noticed far below him his human making his way back to their caravan. He thought he might as well do the same. The battle was over and the chase was done. There might be a chance to wage the war another day, but for the time being this battle was lost.

"I promise," he said. "You have my word."

"Good enough," Barry said and began to descend with great slow flaps of his wings towards Tatton Mere.

31. MEETING

Down on the railway track Luca was amazed and relieved by the intervention of his friend the buzzard. He must have been watching everything from above, Luca thought. And then he thought: good thing it's a full moon and a clear night. He and the squirrels made their way back to where a shocked and shaking Della was standing.

"What on earth was that?" Della said. "What just happened?"

"That was the buzzard," Jimmy said. "We met him earlier. I've heard about the way they work but never seen one in action. They're terrible. Deadly. Death from the sky."

"Good thing this one seems to be on our side then," Jenny said.

Luca explained about his relationship with Barry, and how it was the buzzard who had located the squirrels in the first place.

"Without him, we wouldn't be here now," Luca said.

"Where exactly are we?" Jenny asked.

"And what about Max?" Jimmy said. "What happened to him? Can we go back and see if he's all right?"

"Don't think there's any going back, little feller," Luca said.

They had stopped running along the line and were grouped in a loose circle getting their breath back. The squirrels took the opportunity of the break to get rid of the hateful blue and red collars they were still wearing. Jimmy made short work of Jenny's, and she his.

They were all wondering what to do next. Della noticed they were just next to the big conker tree she had climbed, was it only the previous night? It seemed a lifetime ago. And it was then that Della realised that no one had been introduced. For all the squirrels knew they had been kidnapped by strangers again.

"I think the first thing we should do is all introduce ourselves," Della said. "I'm Della. I know Max and I think I'm a friend of his."

Jimmy of course realised that this was the cat that he had asked Max to do something about. And now she was one of the good guys? Oh well, the world had moved on very quickly it seemed since he was last in Max's garden. He'd ask Max all about it the next time he saw him.

"And I'm a friend of Della's," Luca said. "Rescuing you was Max's idea. We helped."

Just then there came a whoosh from above them and Barry came decelerating down with a great whirl and flutter of wings to finish up standing next to them.

"Hello," he said to Della and the squirrels. "I'm Barkan. I'm a buzzard." He paused. "But you can call me Barry."

Jimmy stared at the buzzard in complete and wide-eyed awe.

Barry passed on the news about everything he'd seen from above.

"The now very wet small dog has given up the chase and is on his way home. The human has given up too and is likewise making his way home. The two big dogs are dead or dispersed. No one's after you now. They've all given up. I think you've made it." And then, best of all as far as the other animals were concerned: "Oh yes. And there's another dog further back along the railway. He's trying to catch you up. He fought the two other bigger dogs in a terrible battle. He won but I think he may be injured. He's limping badly and the human shot him with the gun."

"We better wait then," Jimmy said. "Please."

The others agreed. They stood and stared back along the track the way they had come.

Luca took the opportunity to ask Barry how come he was out and about? Why had he managed to be there just when they needed him?

"It was the little ones!" Barry said. "Always hungry and always clamouring for more. I don't remember being like that at all when I was small."

Luca looked at him in disbelief.

"They got hungry during the night," Barry continued. "And Beryl thought I should see if I could find a juicy night-snack for them, it being a full moon. I was cruising over the fields by the town and heard a great commotion below. That's when I saw you running down the road being chased by the long-haired dogs, the small dog and the fat human. I stuck around. You know, just in case I could help."

He fell silent, and all the animals now looked in the distance for their lost companion. As they looked, for a long moment there was nothing. The long moment stretched into a while.

Waiting for Max

Then the sharper-eyed buzzard said: "He's coming."
The others could still see nothing. Then in the flat distance of

the track Della noticed something white that was bobbing up and down. She couldn't make it out what it was, and tried to focus on it harder. Then she realised it was the white flash on Max's chest and neck she was seeing, bobbing up and down as he hopped along.

"Yes. He's coming," she said.

Now they all could see him clearly in the moonlight. Slowly but steadily coming their way.

Jimmy was close to tears; Jenny felt a surge of relief; Della had a lump in her throat.

Even the world-weary and chase-hardened Luca felt himself surprisingly short of breath as he watched the wounded and battered warrior-dog make his way slowly towards them.

He spoke for them all as Max approached.

"Are we glad to see you, feller," he said.

Jimmy and Jenny were leaping in the air and dancing round Max and chirping wildly and play-fighting each other in their excitement.

Della just said "Yes we are Max. Very much."

Only the polite Barry the buzzard stood to one side and said nothing. He looked hard at the dog. He'd been right about the damage. If anything he'd underestimated it. The dog was in a really bad way. There was blood all over his head, particularly on the left side. In fact, the blood was the best part of it because it masked the real damage underneath. But there were some clear and horrible wounds that Barry could see. One ear seemed to have completely disappeared. There were great gouged furrows running all the way down his head from his neck to his eyebrows. Some of those furrows were dug in pretty deep. There were smaller strips of deep toothmarks running the other way across his head, from where one ear had been right across to the other ear. His right foot was pulped and mangled in a bloody mess.

Max greeted all his friends. "I'm glad to see you too," he said. "I'm okay," he said. "Looks worse than it really is. So far so good."

Luca was the animal there most familiar with injury. He too, like Barry, thought in fact that Max's injuries might actually be worse than they looked. He reckoned Max probably might be losing too much blood to survive the night. Well, he thought, if he's going to die, he'd probably prefer to do it at home. So better get moving then. And if Max died on the way home, then so be it.

Max looked around, as though seeking something.

"What happened to the little yapper?" He said. "I was concerned he might cause serious trouble but I'd get here too late to help."

"Barry sorted him out," Luca said, indicating the buzzard.

Max said hello to the buzzard. They introduced themselves formally.

"We owe you a lot," Max said. "Perhaps I can do something for you?"

"Let's talk about that another time," Barry said. "When you're safely home."

"Talking of which," Luca interrupted. "We should get going. Keep moving."

"And I have to get back to the job I'm supposed to be out doing," Barry said. "They'll be wondering where I've got to." He prepared to rise into the sky, spread his wings and took off.

"Get home safely," he called out of the darkness above.

Luca looked at Max. "We've a long way to go. As you know. How are you feeling?" Meaning, Max knew, do you think you'll hold us up? How far do you think you'll get? And do you think you'll make it?

"I'll keep going," he said. "Come what may." Then added very quietly: "I want to go home."

Della was deeply touched by this hopelessly brave and almost indestructible dog at last asking his friends for help.

"We'll get you there," she said. "We'll get you home Max."

32. AMBUSH

They set off again. Luca and Della now leading the way. Behind them the two squirrels kept pace with Max, who walked and hopped along steadily on three legs.

It didn't turn out to be a bad arrangement. There was no way the two squirrels could normally keep up the pace set by the bigger animals. They were great little sprinters, used to rapidly hurtling across a dangerous open space before reaching the sanctuary of a nearby tree. They were not designed for a long night's route march along a deserted railway line.

Yet now with Max's speed severely curtailed by his injuries, Jimmy and Jenny found they could keep going for long periods at the same speed as Max, bounding and jumping along beside him. It also gave Jimmy a nice feeling that he was protecting Max in some way by walking along with him by his side.

Luca and Della waited every mile or so for the other three to catch them up. They'd take a break and have a drink. Then push on again.

While the others were just glad to be safe and relatively sound, and to be on their way home at last, it was Luca who, as usual, was thinking ahead and going through in his mind the problems they might encounter on the route home. Though they were making good progress, and Luca was astonished how Max kept going, weak as he was, it was clearly going to take them much longer to get back home than it had to get to Knutsford. Luca knew they would lose the cover of darkness and it would be well into the day and broad daylight before they arrived home. If they made it. There would be trains too.

Something else Luca knew from his travels along the line, which the others didn't, was that after a certain time in the day, quite early in the morning, the stations got busy with humans. The trains stopped at these places and the humans climbed aboard or got off. Passing through busy stations might be a problem. He realised that where possible they'd have to go round the stations. If they could.

They pressed on, hour after hour, slow mile after slow mile.

Luca and Della out in front; Max and the squirrels some way behind. At first Max and Jimmy and Jenny chatted a good deal about all that had happened since they had last seen each other. Max was astonished at the Great Squirrel Race and what the squirrels had to do just to get food. Jimmy and Jenny were in turn astonished and amazed that Max had been determined to rescue them. Jimmy was astounded at the effectiveness of the buzzard and how he had located them. But as time went by and the miles eaten up, Max fell more and more silent and talked no more. The squirrels could see he was putting every bit of effort he had left into keeping going. He didn't have the energy to talk any more. They too fell silent and kept him company.

So the animals made their way slowly and steadily along the moonlit track. Della and Luca leading, Max and the squirrels some way behind. The cat and the fox slowly increased their lead over the other three animals, and when it was too far for Luca's comfort, he and Della would wait for the others to come back in sight before moving off again. Sometimes they waited for Jimmy, Jenny and Max to catch up completely. Then they would all stop, take a rest, have a drink; and Luca would take a quick scan of Max to assess how he was doing. He was in a terrible state. Luca could not understand how he kept going. It seemed it was on willpower alone. After a few minutes they would all set off again, but quite soon Della and Luca would be on their own some way in front and the other three some way behind.

Luca was just about to call a halt to Della and let the others catch up again when a voice came out of the shadows on the left and three black shapes slid out of the dark and blocked their way.

"A fox is it now, white lovely? You are one for surprises aren't you?"

It was the tomcat from the night before. This time he had two associates with him. Della could see one was a slightly smaller and stringier version of the big black and white tom, while the other one was a large and broad marmalade striped tom with a chunk missing from one ear. The three cats blocked their route ahead.

"Uh-oh," Luca said quietly to Della. "Tricky bit. See if you can get on the far side of them while I distract them. And run like hell if you have to. We'll circle back and rejoin the others later."

Then addressing the large black and white tom, clearly the leader of this trio of ne'er-do-wells, he said: "Come on mate, what's the problem? Live and let live. Pass and let pass, eh?"

"I've got no beef with you, red friend. None at all. You can go your way as easily as you like. It's your white acquaintance there I want a nice long conversation with. And her dog friend. Have you seen the dog?"

"A dog? Can't say I have," Luca said, giving nothing away. Suddenly he raised his voice: "Quick, quick, watch it, there's a train," he said looking over the cat's shoulder into the distance. Then as they looked back along the track to the non-existent approaching train he darted to one side, distracting all three cats. Della took the opportunity to nip past the obstructing cats on the other side and halted on the track just past them.

"That's the way it is, is it?" said the tom. "In this together are you? Then I'm afraid you're going to get it in the neck now 'friend'."

The tom's two associates closed in on the fox, while the big black and white tom turned round to confront Della.

"Oi, darling, where d'you think you're going?" the tom said. "I didn't give anyone permission to go anywhere. You move on my say-so. Now then, as it happens the lads here will just sort out this foxy red friend of yours and teach him some manners, while me and--"

He never finished what he was going to say. At that moment the huge jaws of the bull terrier caught him low on the back of the neck from above and behind. The totally startled tomcat shrieked wildly and was then instantly lifted and swung right off his feet. The dog gripped the cat's entire neck in the vice of his jaws. He jerked the cat one way, then jerked him back the other. Then faster and faster, even exhausted and battered as he was, he ragged the big cat side to side with incredible speed. There was a sickening clack from the cat's neck as its head was forced to go one in one direction in the air while his body was forced in the other. The big cat went limp.

Having broken the cat's neck and severed its spinal cord, the bull terrier contemptuously flung the body aside. The cat was dead before it landed a few feet away on a concrete sleeper.

"He talked too much," Max said.

He flexed his legs, standing square on both front feet, and just ignored the searing pain from his mangled foot. He turned and prepared to take the fight to the other two cats who were about to attack Luca in a pincer movement from either side. The fox was crouching down low, ready to leap up or aside and escape if and when he could.

"Leave the fox alone," Max said. "Deal with me."

The cats stared at the dog, then looked at each other, then back at the dog steadily advancing towards them, then glanced at each other again. Then simultaneously they both turned and fled into the bushes at the side of the track. The death of their leader opened up new and exciting possibilities in the gang structure among the semi-feral cats in this neighbourhood and neither cat wanted to tangle with this appalling deadly battlecruiser of a dog when there were coups to stage and takeovers to explore and new gang hierarchies to establish.

The line was empty and quiet again and the way ahead clear.

Jimmy and Jenny had kept well back, out of the way, as the bigger animals talked and argued and confronted each other, and had watched as Max had advanced silently and unnoticed until he was just behind the big tomcat, who was talking loudly. Now they joined the others again.

Della for her part was truly staggered by what she had just witnessed. She'd thought, when she saw Max approaching behind the tomcat, that he would somehow frighten the cat and drive it off, like he'd done before. She hadn't really thought he would just kill it. She killed, often, of course she did. But when she killed it was always driven by the thought of food. Even when she wasn't hungry, her killing was always driven by a food instinct. But it was very different with this dog. She never killed so quickly and mechanically as this dog. Nor so matter-of-factly. The big tomcat was a problem. So the dog had just killed him coldly and instantly with absolute efficiency. And then equally instantly he just moved on to the next thing without further thought. The big cat was now dead to him, not just physically but in his mind as well.

Luca inclined his head in thanks to Max for his timely intervention. But Max now sank to the ground and lay down on the track, his snout resting on his front paws.

"I think maybe I need a few minutes to recover my strength." He closed his eyes.

The others waited, saying nothing. Jimmy and Jenny came and sat alongside Max. Luca wondered if this was finally the end for the dog. But after five minutes Max opened his eyes and got back on his feet, a little unsteadily.

"Right," he said. "Let's go home."

He began hobbling and limping along the track. For a long time he said nothing more.

They carried on together under the moonlight.

The first two stations came and went while it was still dark, and there was no problem there. The buildings were still deserted and the animals just kept walking along the side of the track under the face of the platform all the way through to the other side. But by the time they reached a point still some way from the third station it was getting light. This was a town station, not a country halt. Lights were on in the station buildings, and humans were already standing on the platforms. The first trains came along in both directions. The animals hid in the long grass by the side of the track as the trains passed.

Now they faced the problem of getting to the far side of the busy town station in full daylight.

Fortunately in a way, even this relatively busy town station was a shadow of its former self. The busy ticket office buildings and the platforms either side of the line were surrounded by semi-derelict buildings, sheds and warehouses. There were also empty and unused rail sidings, where rusting track maintenance machinery on rusting steel wheels stood against the rusting and rotting buffers. There were quite extensive marshalling yards stretching some distance either side of the station, where in days gone by shunting engines would arrange and re-arrange the goods wagons that carried much material in the days before cheap road transport destroyed the transport of goods and wares by rail. There was an engine turntable that hadn't been used since steam locomotives last pulled the carriages on this line back in the late 1950s. There were other platforms and related station buildings dating from a time when trains ran far more frequently than their current one train an hour. These platforms had trees and shrubs growing from cracks in the unmaintained surfaces. And the buildings were much dilapidated and the windows broken.

All this dereliction provided excellent cover for the travelling rescue party. Some way before they reached the station Luca led them along a side line that followed a route behind the busy central area. They walked head high through weeds growing out of the hard ash-compacted soil. The steel rails and ballast had been removed long before. They rejoined the track a hundred yards after the station.

Easier than I feared, Luca thought.

Next came the high elevated section along the Arches. It was now full daylight.

"No need to rush now, I think," Luca said. "Let's just carry on across."

The great structure that had seemed such a fearsome and serpentine monster in the rain and dark two days before now did not seem so bad. They crossed the forty-seven-legged monster without incident.

And then they were on the last leg before home!

They passed by another busy station by slipping silently behind the ticket office and the closed and abandoned public lavatory building, and came back on the track under the cover of the relative darkness of a road bridge passing overhead. They pressed on, now altogether side by side in a compact group.

Max, who had been silent for the past two hours suddenly lifted up his nose and sniffed the air.

"Home!" he said. "I can smell it."

And very soon the others too began to recognise certain landmarks, and they too realised they were all but home.

They entered the long deep railway cutting that cut across the bottom of the land of their respective homes. Not far now. They'd made it at last. They were home.

33. SHOT

Thirteen-year old Carl Gordon, the TV gardener's boy, was out that morning too, armed with his beloved and by now trusty Walther. He'd been prowling the roads and fields around his father's property with considerable success for a number of weeks. Not a few farm and domestic animals had been killed or maimed. And now he had been patrolling the railway line for the last couple of days or so now looking for animals of various sizes on which to try the gun. And yes, he'd found it could kill cats. It made short work of hedgehogs. And it did serious damage to smaller dogs. But what now attracted him to the line, and what he thought he might see if he was quiet and careful and behaved like a hunter, was a badger or two.

He'd seen a TV documentary recently which said that railway cuttings and embankments were becoming favourite places for badger setts. He thought if he was quiet and careful and behaved like a hunter he would locate a badger sett and try the Walther out on them. He'd also found that there was a time, after dawn, but when it was full light that was the best time. It was animal time, before humans came to dominate the day, when the night animals were returning to their dens and the day animals were first stirring. It was a good time to kill.

And prize of prizes; just yesterday his dad had managed to get hold of the special telescopic sight that was made for the Walther. He hadn't tried the scope yet. He was desperate to use it.

With badgers on his mind, Carl was astonished then that morning to see a group of animals he least expected to see at the bottom of the railway cutting. A cat, a fox, two squirrels and a very battered looking dog.

Stealthily and silently he rested the Walther in the crook of the trunk and a branch of a sycamore sapling growing near the top of the cutting. He examined each animal in turn through the telescopic sight.

He was about a hundred and twenty yards from the animal group. It would be a long shot, a very long shot indeed. But he was sure he could do it. The question was: which one to hit? Which one to take out?

A fox, now that might be good. He'd never hit a fox before. He examined the fox in the crosshairs of the scope. But then, maybe not; it wasn't much bigger than a cat. And he'd seen plenty of times what damage the Walther did to a cat. He was slightly bored by that. The cat then? No point: likewise boring. The squirrels: forget it: done that: killed too many of them already: no mystery there. Boring doesn't touch half of it. That left the dog. He gave the dog a good long hunter's eyed stare through the telescopic sight.

Yes, Carl thought. Nice. Medium sized and very beefy. Who's a good boy then? You're the one today.

While he had been assessing his targets, the animals had gone from view, having left the track, and were now hidden by the brambles and long grass of the cutting, as they made their way up the side of the deep sloping bank to the crest. They would emerge in a moment or two on the flat top of the cutting by the broken-down iron fence. When they did he would be ready for them.

As always, Max brought up the rear. Luca and Della reached the top first, followed by the two squirrels. They ducked under the iron fence and stopped, hidden in and under the bushes in Max's garden. Max stood on the top of the railway cutting. He was exhausted. He was badly wounded and had lost a lot of blood. He felt very faint and slightly dizzy and disoriented. The remnant of his ear sang a monotonous song. His head throbbed and his foot hurt a lot.

Carl had him right in the cross hairs of the scope. He was aiming for a head shot. He held his breath and gently squeezed the trigger.

Some sixth sense, perhaps some notion that he was being watched, made Max turn his head to the right. Either that, or molecules of Carl's scent had drifted on the air to Max's sensitive nose and Max turned his head slightly to catch more of the incoming information. Whichever it was that made Max turn his head, the air rifle slug that would have caught him just above his right cheekbone instead passed through his left eye. The eye was completely destroyed by the slug, which went on to lodge in the bone at the far corner of the eye socket.

Max yelped and staggered forward, fresh blood pouring down

and covering the dried and caked streaks on the left side of his head. He took a series of faltering steps, passing right through the belt of bushes, past where his friends were waiting for him, and out into the open on the lawn. Then utterly exhausted and damaged beyond the extraordinary limits of even his iron constitution, steadfast will, and tireless ability to keep going, he collapsed and lay still.

34. DREAMLAND

Max dreamed again. He was in some kind of strange-smelling clean very bright room. He wasn't dead, he knew that. He could feel all his injuries, but somehow they didn't feel as dangerous as they had done before. In a way it seemed his injuries were ebbing away. They hadn't got him this time. He was mending, he was sure of it. There would be permanent damage, he knew that, but he'd be all right. After all, many bull terriers had known worse, his mum always told him when he hurt himself as a pup.

He drifted in and out of consciousness, and dreamed.

When he'd emerged from the bushes and collapsed on the lawn, he was seen immediately by one of his humans. She was in the kitchen standing at the kitchen sink staring sightlessly out of the kitchen window wondering worriedly what had become of their beloved Max. He'd been missing for nearly two days now, and there was no sign of him. Had he been stolen? Had he been kidnapped and sold to a dog-fighting ring? That was a real worry. Oh poor Max, she thought. We'll never see you again.

And then unbelievably there was a stir in the bushes on the other side of the lawn above the railway line and Max staggered out and collapsed on the lawn. She shouted for her husband and rushed outside.

Both humans knelt down by Max's side.

"He's in a bad way," one of the humans said. "He's got some terrible injuries. Terrible. Look at that. Unbelievable."

"It looks like he's been fighting," the other human said. "Has he been made to fight d'you think?"

"Could be. He's still breathing though. Still alive but we better get him to the vet fast."

And so while one human rushed back inside the house to phone the vet, the other carefully lifted the unconscious Max and carried him to a car, laid him down gently on a rug on the back seat, and hurtled away.

At the vet's Max was taken immediately into emergency surgery. Two veterinary surgeons worked for three hours to save Max's life and repair what they could of the damage he had received.

When they finished, one of the surgeons phoned Max's humans.

"We've operated," he said. "He's in recovery now. It'll be touch and go for a while yet. He's lost a lot of blood. He's also lost an eye. And one ear has completely gone."

"Was it from fighting?" Max's human asked. "Has he been in a dogfight?"

"Yes and no," the surgeon said. "There were definitely injuries caused by a dog or dogs. His right paw has been badly chewed, and a bone in his foot is broken in two places, probably by a dog; and there was also some superficial teeth damage to his head. But none of those injuries was really bad."

"Oh, that's odd," Max's human interrupted. "What did the serious damage then?"

"A shotgun," the surgeon replied. "And also, and separately we think, a shot from a powerful air rifle. That's what blinded his left eye."

"What!" the human said. "Unbelievable."

"Ask him if he's going to be okay," Max's other human said, listening in on the conversation. "Ask him."

"Is he going to be all right?"

"It's really too early to say," the surgeon replied. "I'm sorry but it really is. The surgery was a success. We've removed all the shotgun pellets, and the air rifle slug. And we've cleaned up the eye and the ear and the deep cuts on his head. And where there was bone damage, we've cleaned all that up too. And we've x-rayed his foot, cleaned it and stitched it up, and he's got a tight splint-bandage on that now holding the breaks in place.

"In a way all that's the easy part. But the recovery period can be as dangerous to some animals as the initial damage and the surgery. He's taken a hell of a battering. We'll have to see how he does over the next two weeks. We've patched him up as best we can. He's sedated and on a drip now. He's had a blood transfusion. He'll probably need another one. Now it's up to him. Appalling damage, as I said. But bull terriers are amazingly tough. Incredibly robust animals. So I'd say yes. He's lost an eye and an ear. He'll be covered in scars for the rest of his life. But if all goes well and there are no setbacks, I think he'll recover. I think he'll make it."

The veterinary surgeon didn't add that he had recovered the air rifle slug, and had recognised it. He had taken quite a few of this type of unique slug out of domestic animals and pets in the past few weeks. He was beginning to get an idea of the geography of the damage locus, which all seemed to be centred on a particular area. With one particular farm right at the epicentre. And he had a pretty good idea of who lived there, as he had tended to their chocolate labradors for several minor things over the years. He had passed the slugs and all the information he had on the carnage caused by the illegal weapon to the police. He expected them to be making a call on the farm very soon.

There was another course of action the vet was mulling over in his mind. This was to involve the newspapers. This he knew might be more effective in stopping the carnage being wreaked on the local pets by junior Gordon than anything the police and the courts might do such as confiscating the weapon and imposing a fine. There was the great whiff of hypocrisy here in the public pontifications of the grand TV life-preserving conservationist contrasted with the private realities of his son's deadly behaviour. There is nothing the reader of newspapers loves more than hypocrisy. And nothing the papers love more than supplying stories of it. The vet thought he might well be soon on the phone having a chat with the newsdesk of one of the tabloids.

Heavily drugged and bandaged, Max lay sleeping in a stall at the veterinary hospital.

He dreamed.

He dreamed he was his ancestor Jacko. The famous rat-killer Jacko from generations and generations before.

Jacko and other bull terriers killed rats in specially built pits behind pubs where gentlemen and other punters came and watched and cheered and shouted and laid bets on the numbers of dead rats the bull terriers killed in a certain amount of time. And it was Jacko who was champion. Jacko, who once killed one thousand rats in a single non-stop session in the pit, in batches of a hundred a time, with the last hundred rats being despatched in five minutes twenty-eight seconds.

And that dream faded and a new dream came. And in this dream it seemed he was visited by two huge and familiar shapes.

Grey Wolf and Albion. The lean long grey shape seemed to lie on his left, his head on his paws next to Max's head, the blue eyes deep with sadness and melancholy. And the long lean white shape lay on his right, his head on his paws next to Max's head, the red eyes dancing with delight and possibility.

Albion spoke first. His white shape became brighter and the grey form faded slightly. "Hello Max," he whispered inside Max's head. "Look what they've done to you. Humans. Not to be trusted. Ever. They have no honour. They never did. Now's your chance. Go wild. Go feral. Break the contract. And run free."

Then the white form faded a little and the grey shape became fuller and stronger.

"Who brought you here, little dog?" Grey Wolf said. "Who saved your life? They missed you terribly. They searched everywhere for you. They want you well and they want you back. Remember, little dog, the squirrel was right. You don't always have to do what you're supposed to do."

"That's nice," Albion said speaking directly to his brother for the first time. "But it doesn't apply to humans, does it brother? Wouldn't the cruel human boy too benefit from looking at the world that way?"

"Yes, brother, of course," Grey Wolf replied with more than a lifetime of sadness. "Humans are as we find them. We can't make them be what we want them to be. We can't make them perfect. They are what they are."

Max heard the age-long anger in one voice and the generations-long sadness in the other, and knew he had come to a point in his life where he could make a choice between them.

In Max's dream he saw himself becoming a village dog. One of a feral band of dogs that scavenged and lived well enough on rubbish tips. And everyone was equal in the band, there was no false imposed hierarchy like wolves had with their stupid alpha pairs. Everyone could eat when they wanted, and everyone in the gang was equal and could have their say when they had something to say. And the gang steered well clear of humans and had no contact with them. Life with the gang would be exciting and dangerous and interesting and free. And always there, but in the background felt but never seen was the presence of a great white albino wolf. And he was pleased to see his children flourish and do well.

Then that vision faded and Max saw himself back in his garden, pottering about, investigating, talking to his friends. But most importantly he was interacting with humans. They were good and kind to him, and for their part they stuck to the contract their ancestors had made with Grey Wolf all those generations ago. But Max was not free. He was under their control, and had to do as he was bid; and he could only get food when it was given to him. But that was regularly every day.

And though this vision was not as exciting as that laid before him by Albion, Max knew where his heart lay. He would stay on the course laid out by Grey Wolf thirty thousand years before.

In his dream he murmured: "I accept humans for what they are. Both kind and cruel. I won't break the contract. That is my choice."

Immediately with those words the two great wolf shapes faded away. And Max slept. This time for a long while there were no more dreams.

Time and the days passed. Max slept. His bandages were changed regularly. He was given a course of antibiotics to counteract the bacteria that may have come from the teeth of the other dog or dogs. The drip kept him hydrated. And slowly but surely he began to mend. His wounds began to heal. The ringing in his left ear stopped and he began to hear again with the remnants of that ear. The inner and middle ear were intact, it was just the high curved leaf-shaped outer ear that used to stand vertically above his head that had disappeared. The veterinary surgeon had made a neat job of cutting away the vestiges of the shattered ear. He'd also cleaned out the destroyed left eye and sewn the eyelid down over it. Max would be a one-eyed dog for the rest of his life. But he would still be a two-eared dog, even if one of the ears was no longer as easily visible as it used to be. The stitch lines across the top of his head brought the recovering flesh together neatly and red lines of scars were beginning to form there. The bone where it was damaged underneath the flesh was growing and replenishing and knitting again.

And after a week or so of resting and sleeping and recovering, Max began to stir and move around again in his stall. He was getting back on his feet, albeit unsteadily at first.

But for a while in the first days it was touch and go. It was only after the first week and more had gone by that the vet felt able to ring Max's humans and tell them that things looked good.

"I definitely think he's over the worst," he said on the phone. "He's getting quite perky again. In fact," the vet said. "We knew he was on his way to recovery when he started trying to bite his drip."

"We were thinking," Max's human said. "That he may have been kidnapped for a dog-fighting ring. Then he may have escaped. That's when he got shot. Do you think that's possible.?"

"Certainly possible," the vet said. "In my opinion he's definitely been in dog-fights, maybe several. And he was definitely shot, twice. Either at the same time or on two different occasions. We don't know. So who knows? Only the dog knows what he's been through. Perhaps in a way he got lucky."

In his own mind the vet thought the two shootings were unrelated. Different guns meant they were probably done by different people on two different occasions. He was pretty certain the air rifle slug was local. Whereas the shotgun could have happened anywhere. He hadn't heard of any dog-fighting rings in the area, but had no idea about further afield. There were probably plenty of them in Manchester. Until we get like Dr Doolittle, he thought, and can talk to the animals, we'll never know what this dog's been through and how far he's travelled to get back home.

"So be thankful he's back and survived it all and still in one piece," the vet said. "He's a lucky dog I think."

The vet said that if things went according to plan, they could come and take Max home at the end of another week.

35. WAIT

For Max's friends it was a very long two and a half weeks.

Della, Luca, Jimmy and Jenny had heard the shot that had hit Max; they'd seen him stagger past them through the bushes and they'd seen him collapse on the lawn. Jimmy had to be physically restrained by Luca from rushing out on to the lawn to his friend's side.

"Wait, wait, little feller," he said, placing his paw round the squirrel. "You can't. Watch." For Luca had seen movement through the kitchen window.

And sure enough, two humans immediately rushed out of the house and kneeled by the collapsed form of the unconscious Max. The animals watched from the bushes, hardly daring to breathe as Max was lifted up and taken away.

Della was the one of the four there most familiar with human speech. Luca and the two squirrels had no idea of what had been said.

"What did they say?" Jimmy asked her.

"I think they said he was badly injured but was still breathing; that he was still alive," she replied. "I think," she stressed.

"Where've they taken him?" Jimmy asked. "Where's he gone?"

But Della didn't know. She'd been to the same veterinary practice herself for injections and to be de-fleaed, but she didn't know that the same place was also where animals were taken for more serious things.

"I just don't know," she said. "I'm sorry."

"Me neither," Luca said.

"But if he gets better, he'll be back won't he?" Jimmy said.

"I hope so. We all do," Luca said. Though his natural reality-driven melancholia told him they'd never see Max again. But he didn't say that. The squirrels would find out for themselves soon enough. In the meantime there was no harm in letting them hope.

The four friends still stood hidden in the bushes. They knew there was nothing for it now but to go their own ways. They arranged to meet regularly, if they could, then dispersed. Della promised to keep her ears and eyes open and pass on any news she heard about Max to the others. Della returned to her own garden, next to Max's on the other side away from the railway. Luca went back to the railway cutting to head further along to new hunting grounds in the west for a while. After that he planned to head east and spend a couple of days in the company of his old mucker Barry the buzzard. The two squirrels went with him until they came to their old home tree.

"If I can advise you, fellers," Luca said. "It might be a good idea to move home. The humans who kidnapped you might come looking here again. You never know. Never trust a human."

They said their farewells and the squirrels thanked the fox for all he'd done for them. They hoped to see him again soon.

"Look out for me during the dark of the moon," he said and sped away, a red shadow among the ferns and long grass.

The two squirrels were left sitting in the lower branches of their former home tree.

"He's right," Jenny said. "We should move. It's not safe here anymore."

"Where shall we go?"

"Why don't we try to find a place in Max's garden?" Jenny said. "He'll look after us if anyone tries to kidnap us there."

But the days went by and Max did not reappear in the garden.

The squirrels found a dense and untenanted holly tree in a corner of Max's garden and made a safe home there. They saw Della regularly and often met for a chat on top of the high brick wall. She had no news of Max.

Luca too still came through that way on a Tuesday night. And there was always a dead mouse waiting for him on the wall top.

But there was still no sign nor news of Max.

The days stretched to weeks. The squirrels still hoped that Max was recovering somewhere and when he got well he would return and they would see him again. Luca was pretty sure that Max had died of his injuries and they'd never see him again. Della's thought was somewhere in between. She hoped and half-believed; but reason said otherwise.

Then one day Max's humans went away in their car, and about an hour later came back. None of the animals was there to see a heavily bandaged brindled, black and white bull terrier step carefully out of the back seat of the car and with a limp follow his humans into the house.

My name's Max

It was a Tuesday and the friends had arranged to meet that night, on top of the wall, when Luca passed through.

Della was there first. She sat on the wall, cleaning her paws. She'd brought a dead mouse with her and laid it out on the wall. The squirrels jumped up onto the wall a few minutes later.

And then, much earlier than expected Luca the fox joined them on the wall too, with greetings from Barry. They exchanged news. They all hadn't been gathered together since the previous Tuesday, and there were a lot of respective animal things to talk about.

They were so busy talking that none of them noticed a medium-sized black and white and brindled dog make his way, with a limp, through the rhododendrons to the base of the wall below the four animals.

He raised his snout, in shape and profile very reminiscent of the nose of a Messerschmidt Me 109 fighter from the Second World War, and looked at his friends gathered together on the wall. They still hadn't noticed him.

"Hello," he said. "My name's Max. I'm a bull terrier."

The murmur of conversation between the animals on top of the wall stopped instantly. There was a moment of intense silence. Then all kinds of animal hubbub was let loose as all Max's friends jumped down from the wall to be by his side and greet him and welcome him home.

"Well," he said. "Sometimes it's right to do just what you're supposed to."

36. SPECIAL

Tools Tilly never did repeat the success he'd had with the first Great Squirrel Race. It turned out in the end to be a one-off. He tried two more pairs of squirrels that Ron and Ray trapped for him, but they just wouldn't do it.

The increasingly desperate Tools sent Ron and Ray out yet again to catch a third pair. It was no good. They just didn't get the hang of what they were supposed to do.

In each case, even with the ferocious Snough (who now had four strange scars on his back that Tools was much perplexed by) telling them they would be deadmeat if they didn't do it, the new squirrels could never be made to run the obstacle course. Eventually Tools was forced to release them back into the wild.

It turned out, though Tools only afterwards fully appreciated it, that Jimmy and Jenny were two very special squirrels indeed.

Mark Moore
55,555 words

Made in the USA
Charleston, SC
05 November 2015